The end of a fairy tale . . .

The Countess Lila Fowler di Mondicci dug her toes into the smooth white sand of the Italian Riviera and looked out to sea. Tisiano was Jet Skiing about a hundred yards offshore. The motor roared above the slap of the waves.

As she watched the green waters of the Mediterranean, Tisiano waved, then expertly jumped the Jet Ski over some rough water. When he had stopped bouncing, he smiled at her and zoomed on.

When Lila looked out at the water again, Tisiano was closer to shore, about fifty yards out. But this time she saw a thin line of blue flame licking along the Jet Ski. That couldn't be—the glare of the setting sun on the water was making her see things. . . .

The explosion rocked the air, hurling bolts of sound across the waves to shake the beach. Lila fell to the ground, partly from concussion and partly from shock. A ball of flame leaped to the sky and raged briefly. Then the sea was calm and green and silent again, only small waves disturbing its glassy surface.

There was no Jet Ski.

There was no Tisiano.

Bantam Books in the Sweet Valley University series
Ask your bookseller for the books you have missed

SWEET VALLEY UNIVERSITY™

Good-bye to Love

Written by
Laurie John

Created by
FRANCINE PASCAL

BANTAM BOOKS
NEW YORK · TORONTO · LONDON · SYDNEY · AUCKLAND

RL 6, age 12 and up

GOOD-BYE TO LOVE

A Bantam Book / October 1994

Sweet Valley High® *and Sweet Valley University*™
are trademarks of Francine Pascal
Conceived by Francine Pascal
Produced by Daniel Weiss Associates, Inc.
33 West 17th Street
New York, NY 10011

ISBN: 0-553-56652-0

Published simultaneously in the United States and Canada

Bantam Books are published by Bantam Books, a division of Bantam
Doubleday Dell Publishing Group, Inc. Its trademark, consisting of the
words "Bantam Books" and the portrayal of a rooster, is Registered in
U.S. Patent and Trademark Office and in other countries. Marca
Registrada. Bantam Books, 1540 Broadway, New York, New York 10036.

PRINTED IN THE UNITED STATES OF AMERICA

OPM   0 9 8 7 6 5 4 3 2 1

To Jordan David Adler

Chapter One

Lila Fowler slipped on her sunglasses and reached for the glass of lemonade on a nearby table. *"Non mi serve niente,"* she said dismissively to the maid.

"Signora," the maid demurred respectfully.

Taking a long drink of lemonade, Lila surveyed her surroundings. A bird sang loudly somewhere in the thick leaves of the tree over her head. The gently rolling green-and-pink hills of Italy stretched before her, fading into hazy blue in the distance. Her chaise and the umbrella table were on a wide stone piazza surrounding an elegant rectangular pool filled with cool blue water.

Lila narrowed her eyes. "So now what?" she asked herself.

Her husband wasn't home to entertain her. As usual, the Count di Mondicci was selling computer parts in France. Computer parts that paid for all this luxury: the villa, pool, wine cellar, and hot-and-cold-running servants.

Before her, the swimming pool sloshed quietly. Lila thought about diving in, but she wasn't quite warm enough yet. She turned on her side to evenly brown her legs, tugging on the edge of her new navy-blue bikini.

"I have the best tan of my life," she muttered. "No wonder—I sit out here about ten hours a day. Tisiano's always away on those stupid business trips."

Lila still felt a little unsure of herself in Italy, even in her own home. *I'm a foreigner,* she thought. *I always will be.* She reached out again and sorted through the pile of books and magazines on the table. There it was: her Sweet Valley High yearbook.

Lila opened it at the middle and smiled at a picture of herself and her best friend, Jessica Wakefield. They had their arms around each other, and were sticking out their tongues at the camera.

We were just kids back then, Lila thought. Still, they'd had a lot of fun.

She flipped through the pages. There was Jessica as homecoming queen, straightening her crown. Lila had been a member of her court and stood beside her. Lila and Jessica filled a lot of the yearbook: they had been the stars of Sweet Valley High.

Frowning, Lila slammed the yearbook shut. Jessica's recent letter to her dropped out of the back.

Lila picked it up and reread it. Pledging the Thetas, the number-one sorority at Sweet Valley University. Dating incredible men and then marrying the pick of the bunch. Parties, football games.

Of course, that was all kid stuff too. Lila was glad she'd had so many real cultural experiences in Italy. For example, she had just gotten back from Venice, where she and Tisiano had sped from artwork to artwork by motorboat taxi.

But Lila was a little tired of culture. And Venice smelled like dead seaweed.

In some ways she had been glad to get away from Sweet Valley. Everyone had her so completely stereotyped there—just changing her hairstyle would have caused a riot. She was tired of the way everyone in Sweet Valley said she was thoughtless and spoiled and went through guys like popcorn.

Her life had begun to bore even her. That was why she'd decided to spend last summer in Italy: to experience some culture and develop meaningful relationships, hopefully with exciting Italian men.

Well, that part of the Great Experiment certainly worked, Lila thought, smiling into her lemonade glass. She had bumped into Tisiano at

3

the Leaning Tower of Pisa, which really did lean at an alarming tilt. Lila had been staring at it, fascinated, wondering who could have made such a dumb mistake in building a tower, when somebody had spoken to her.

"Ciao," he had said, his voice deep and silky.

"Scuzi?" Lila had responded, searching frantically for her phrase book and her composure. Tisiano had straight, thick black hair and brilliant green eyes. He wore a tailored black Italian suit and carried a bulging briefcase made of plush Italian leather. "So you are an American," he'd said softly in English.

"Yes. Yes," Lila had said, as if repeating herself would somehow make her seem mysterious.

"Are you visiting?" he asked with a smile sweeter than Italian apricots. Lila gave up searching for her phrase book.

"No, I live here—sort of. With my aunt. Just for the summer." *Get a grip, Lila,* she scolded herself. *You've talked to guys before.* They had just never had eyes the color of the Mediterranean Sea. "Have you been inside the Tower yet?" she asked, sweeping her long, light-brown hair back over her shoulders.

"No, I am here on business. Natives don't visit the Tower for fun. I am attending a computer convention in Pisa."

"Oh." Lila couldn't think of anything intelligent to say about computers, despite the fact that her father worked in the industry.

"It has been a long day," the gorgeous Italian remarked. "Would you care to accompany me to a café for a cup of espresso or cappuccino?"

"I'd be delighted," Lila drawled, finding her old self. *Yes!* she screamed inside. *This is what I came to Italy for.*

"By the way, I am Count Tisiano di Mondicci," he said with another flashing smile.

"Lila Catherine Fowler," said Lila, suppressing a squeal. Wait till she wrote Jessica about her coffee with a count!

Tisiano led her to a small, quaint café with a blue awning. They sat at a table for two, facing the street. Groups of American tourists in Hawaiian shirts wandered by, talking loudly. A few slim, dark Italians in suits, perhaps colleagues of Tisiano's, walked quickly past.

The waiter hurried over to them. *"Desidera qualcosa?"* he asked.

"Mi porta un cappuccino?" Lila said sweetly, trying to keep a note of triumph out of her voice.

Tisiano smiled appreciatively. Lila smiled back. All those hours she'd spent on the plane cramming Italian phrases were paying off. Obviously Tisiano was impressed. She was already plotting how she would see him again.

Tisiano said in an authoritative voice: *"Mi porti un cappuccino."*

"Grazie, signore." The waiter hurried off.

"Now we can people-watch." Tisiano sat forward. "Or maybe I will just watch you. You are very beautiful."

Lila could feel herself blushing. She had been complimented by tons of guys, of course, but never by an Italian count who looked like Alec Baldwin, Jason Priestley, and Christian Slater all rolled in one.

His green eyes held hers.

"I have a villa near Genoa and an apartment in Rome," he went on. "I return to the villa tonight. That is where I call home. Why don't you"—he reached for her hands—"why don't you visit me there? It is only about a hundred miles by train. I know my invitation is abrupt, but"—he stopped to drink her in with those eyes—"Italian men can be victims of sudden and violent emotions."

Of course Lila had agreed to go, the very next week. She did have to overcome a few obstacles first.

The first obstacle was that her aunt expected Lila to stay with her for the entire summer. That was related to the second obstacle: if Lila left her aunt's house for a few days, Lila's parents would find out.

Lila had no idea what would happen then. Her parents might be cool about it—after all, Lila was eighteen years old and ought to be al-

6

lowed to make her own decisions. But her father might forget that, hop the first plane to Genoa, and show up on the doorstep with a shotgun.

Lila couldn't imagine telling her aunt about her plans. Aunt Maria—a distant relation of her father's—was an Italian aunt out of the movies: gaunt and darkly forbidding. She lectured Lila almost daily on the perils of losing her virginity before the age of ninety.

Without meaning to, though, Aunt Maria had encouraged Lila to pursue the count. She had told plenty of stories about the di Mondicci family. They were extremely wealthy, and were well-known in all of Italy.

So Lila had just said good-bye and left for Genoa. Her parents had remained cool, or at least where they were. And six short weeks later she was the Countess di Mondicci.

The maid reappeared, startling Lila out of her reverie, and said something in Italian. Lila waved her off again and picked up her cordless phone. *I'll call Jess,* she thought. *I need to talk to someone who really understands.*

But before Lila could dial, the gate to the wrought-iron fence around the villa clanged. Lila shaded her eyes with her hand and looked down the drive. Tisiano! He was back!

Lila jumped up from the chaise, automatically combing her fingers through her hair. *But I don't have to worry about how I look,* she thought as her heart began to pound. *Tisiano loves me for my soul, just like I love him for his.*

The deep-blue Ferrari stopped abruptly in a spray of gravel. Tisiano leaped over the side. "Lila!" he cried. "My darling, my love, my life! Oh, I've missed you! But see what I have brought—finery for my countess."

As Lila ran to him, Tisiano dropped his armload of packages. A diamond necklace slipped out of its box onto the gravel. He took Lila in his arms and kissed a quick, frantic circle around her face.

"I have never been more miserable," he said breathlessly. "Without you, I don't have a reason for living. Every day at that stupid conference seemed to last forever. I don't want to travel without you again."

Happiness surged through Lila like the incoming tide. She looked into Tisiano's stunning green eyes and laughed. "You're adorable, *ciao mio!*" she cried, throwing her arms around his neck.

What could I possibly be missing at SVU that's better than this? she thought.

At Sweet Valley University, Jessica Wakefield sat up very straight at her desk. She reached for her philosophy book and placed it squarely in front of her.

Then she leaned over to check her appearance in the large wall mirror. *Yep, that's me, all right,* Jessica thought dryly. Long, golden-blond hair with bangs, blue-green eyes, heart-shaped face, dimple in the left cheek. Behind her, Jessica could also see the rest of the room.

Her twin sister Elizabeth's desk was empty. She was probably outside, enjoying the mild, sunny Sunday afternoon, flirting with guys. Jessica frowned at the irony. Here she was, stuck inside, planning to study all afternoon. It was a total role reversal. They might be identical twins, but Elizabeth had always been the hardworking, dependable sister, while Jessica partied the days and nights away.

"I like studying." Jessica said her affirmation into the mirror. If she repeated it another thousand times, it might actually become true.

Then Jessica tore herself away from the mirror, took a deep breath, and looked at her philosophy book. A photo of a grim man with a mustache hovered over the text. *What is called thinking?* the philosopher wanted to know.

Jessica sighed. Lately, she knew too much about what was called thinking. More than she had ever wanted to know.

But what else can I do? she thought. *I'm still married to Mike, a man who's paralyzed. My brother Steven is a wreck because he has to take care of Mike. What can I do but think about it?*

It was all her fault. Her whole brief marriage

9

had been a total disaster, and it had really made her look long and hard at her life. It was clear she had to change her ways. From now on, she planned to study ten hours a day and make sure she hung out only with girls.

"I want to make my parents proud of me," she said firmly. "And I want to be proud of myself, too. I made some big mistakes, but I'm a new woman now."

A bell rang in the quad. Jessica got up, went over to the window, and squinted out into the December sunshine. It was so bright that she could hardly see. Maybe she would need glasses soon. Well, that would fit her new image.

Jessica scowled.

Almost directly below her window, the Theta Alpha Theta sorority was holding a bake sale. Jessica knew most of the members, because she had pledged the Thetas at the beginning of the semester. A poster announced in large letters that the money raised from the bake sale would go to a shelter for battered women and children.

Jessica noticed that the Thetas had help. Sitting in a makeshift booth were some members of the Sigma fraternity. Actually, Jessica realized, they weren't just any Sigmas. They were the ones in the worst trouble with the school authorities over the secret-society scandal Elizabeth had exposed. They were neatly dressed and wholesome-looking, obviously trying to improve their image. Jessica snorted.

Some of the Thetas were running around the quad, trying to charm other students into buying goodies. Occasionally Alison Quinn, vice president of the Thetas, would ring a silver bell so that people would take notice of the sale—and her.

Jessica propped her elbows on the windowsill and rested her chin on her hands, feeling an old interest stir. *I wonder if I'm completely dead with the Thetas. I definitely used to be their type.*

Behind her, the thick stack of books waited on her desk. She couldn't think about the Thetas when she had so much studying to do. She had failed or missed more tests than she cared to remember, first because of her romance with Mike, then because of the trouble with him. Even if she got solid A's in all her courses for the rest of the semester, she'd be lucky if she averaged C's for final grades. What was the point in even trying?

Jessica sat down at her desk. "The point is not to flunk out," she told herself sternly.

She pushed aside the grim philosopher and reached for her chemistry book, the biggest book in the stack. The cover showed blue and red balls zinging through space. Jessica opened the book and frowned.

"Chemistry *may be defined as the science that is concerned with the characterization, composi-*

tion, and transformations of matter," she read. "That definition, however, is far from adequate."

It was adequate enough to put Jessica to sleep. She groaned. "Why did I take chemistry, anyway?" she muttered, although she knew the answer. The old Jessica had thought there would be a lot of cute premeds in that class.

Actually, there were. Jessica settled back in her desk chair and gazed at the ceiling. Especially one Future Doctor of America who always sat in the front row. He had never seemed to notice her. But then, she had never tried to make him notice her. Jessica had been so distracted by her problems with Mike that she hadn't even found out the doctor-to-be's name, and here it was nearly the end of the semester.

Jessica realized she was daydreaming. "How can you think about him?" she scolded herself. "Haven't you had enough trouble? And it's not over yet, even though the semester almost is."

The Christmas holidays were coming soon. Elizabeth would be bringing Tom Watts home with her for Christmas; he was an orphan or something tragic like that. Jessica made a face.

Tom did have a nice bod. Maybe that was why Elizabeth had spent almost every night since the beginning of the semester closeted at the TV station with him. During the day Jessica had seen the two of them roaming the campus playing boy and girl reporter.

12

Then last week Elizabeth had flipped out. Jessica couldn't help grinning at the memory. All her life Elizabeth had gone for nice, stable, serious relationships—good grief, she'd been with Todd Wilkins all through high school. But now that she and Tom had finally discovered they were in love, Elizabeth had developed a new personality. She went around humming and sighing and forgetting everything. Her desk was covered with dust because she hadn't studied in days. It was unnerving. Kind of humorous, but unnerving.

Jessica thought about Christmas again, tugging her hair in exasperation.

Great—I can't wait. Elizabeth and Tom will be stuck together like old bubblegum, whispering sickeningly sweet things to each other, and I'll be alone. A third wheel, she thought unhappily. For the first time in her eighteen years, she didn't have a guy, any guy—not since Mike had agreed to the annulment of their marriage. Sometimes the loneliness was almost more than she could bear. Nobody understood how she felt.

Lila might have understood. But she was living across a couple of oceans with her Italian husband and would probably never be back. Jessica hadn't written Lila in weeks, not since right after she and Mike were married.

At first she had bragged to Lila about her great college life, trying to make it sound every bit as exciting and glamorous as being an Italian countess. Then, when everything had fallen apart with Mike, the Thetas, and even her dumb waitress job, Jessica hadn't wanted to tell anyone about it who didn't have to know.

But Lila *was* a married woman. Even if she was happily married, she might be able to imagine how it felt to lose a husband. She might actually have some worthwhile advice to give Jessica about what she should do now.

Jessica pushed the chem book aside and took a piece of stationery out of her desk drawer.

> *Dear Lila,*
> *I know I haven't written in a long time. It's not just because I'm always bad about writing letters.*
> *I have big news. I'm not even sure how to tell you this. Basically, my dream marriage with Mike turned into a nightmare.*

Jessica stopped to wipe away a tear. She remembered how Mike had been when she first met him. His sensuous mouth, his thick, unruly dark hair. His strong arms that had held her so passionately and close at night. They had been serious right from the start. He had even been her very first—and only—lover.

A wave of misery washed over her. Jessica stood and walked slowly to her dresser. She

14

opened the top drawer and groped under a pile of sweaters.

There it was, cold and heavy. Jessica fished out her silver wedding ring and held it in her trembling hand. Another tear splashed on the dresser.

She set down the ring at the top of the stationery and picked up her pen.

He got very possessive and demanding, and I guess I just didn't want to be tied down. So we had a lot of fights, and then a completely horrible one. It was so bad I ran to Steven's apartment and hid, but Mike came after me with a gun. I know it sounds incredible. While Mike and Steven were fighting, the gun went off. Mike accidentally shot himself . . .

Jessica had practically had to be dragged to the hospital to see Mike. He had looked terrifying, surrounded by beeping, blinking machines and connected to an army of black tubes. His arms were bruised purple from the tubes, which the doctors were using to medicate and feed him. He had lost a tremendous amount of weight.

Jessica closed her eyes. Sometimes she wished that she had never gone to visit Mike. Now she would always picture him the way he had been

15

in the hospital—permanently damaged by what she had done to him. It would have been better if he had screamed at her for ruining his life. Instead, he had said he loved her, and he had set her free. Now she was left with nothing but guilt.

Jessica shook her head, trying to banish the painful memories. Then she got up and shoved the wedding ring back under the sweaters in her drawer. Back at her desk, she crumpled the piece of stationery, then reached for her chemistry book.

"I don't want to go," Steven Wakefield muttered, setting down his coffee cup.

At the stove, Billie set down a pot hard in irritation. "I'm so tired of hearing you complain," she said, shaking her head. Her forehead was creased in a frown.

Steven's lips tightened. They were fighting about the same thing they'd been fighting about for the last three months—Mike McAllery. Billie wouldn't even look at him.

What is with you? Steven wanted to say, but he didn't. "I only meant"—he cleared his throat—"that it's going to be really hard for me to help Mike with his rehabilitation. He was acting OK at first after the accident, but yesterday at the hospital . . ."

"What?" Billie asked impatiently, starting to

put dishes away so roughly that Steven was afraid they would shatter.

"Now he's decided it's my fault he got shot," Steven said. "I mean, I guess it's my fault the gun went off, since we were fighting, but he's the one who actually shot himself. And he's the one who came here looking for trouble."

"Looking for Jessica," Billie corrected, finally turning around. "You know, she *was* his wife. He was wrong to threaten her, but she did her best to drive him nuts. She married him, then ran away from him every chance she got. Then she finally ran away from him to *you*."

"I'm her big brother—of course she came to me. But it's not fair for Mike to blame me for what happened," Steven said.

"Being paralyzed for life isn't fair either, Steven. Maybe you could show a little sympathy." Billie sat at the kitchen table and buried her face in the newspaper.

Billie always liked Mike, Steven thought, feeling his anger rising. *Even though he spent all his time chasing women and riding that damn motorcycle. She's still on his side.*

"What is your problem?" he demanded. "Just what do you think I should have done?"

"Do you really want to hear it again?" Billie asked, throwing down the paper. "You spent the last month watching Mike out the window and following him around, as if that would somehow protect Jessica. I'm sure Mike really enjoyed that. But it was even more fun for me. Any girl would like having her boyfriend put his sister first."

"All that's over now," Steven said. He felt stupid and irritated. Why was she being so sarcastic?

"So what's the plan for today?" Billie asked coldly.

"I have to go help Mike," Steven said wearily. "That about sums up my day."

Billie gave him an exasperated look, then stood and walked into the bedroom.

Steven shook his head. The judge had sentenced him to help Mike every day until he could take care of himself. Steven couldn't imagine how that would help either of them.

He stuck his head around the bedroom door. Billie had her back to him, standing in front of the closet they shared. Hands on her hips, she was staring at the clothes hanging neatly there.

"Well—I'll see you later," he said.

Silence. Steven sighed and let himself out of their apartment. Mike McAllery lived just one flight below Steven and Billie, and Steven wished wholeheartedly that the trip would take longer. He felt as if he were going to his own execution, but he might as well get this over with.

He banged on Mike's door. "McAllery!"

No answer. Steven sighed and put his key in the lock. The door swung open into gloom. The place gave Steven the creeps. Even though Mike couldn't walk, somehow Steven almost expected him to jump out from the shadows.

The kitchen was as clean as a hospital's. Steven glanced into the living room. No sign of life.

Feeling annoyed, Steven marched to the bedroom. He hated being in this room. It was where Mike had entertained all his women—including Jessica.

Mike lay under a rumpled and dingy pile of covers, listening to a Walkman. His wheelchair was upended in a corner of the room. The floor was littered with dirty glasses, motorcycle magazines, and used tissues. Seeing Mike so helpless still made Steven almost sick with pity.

"Get out of bed," he said briskly, striding to the window and yanking up the blinds.

Mike grunted.

"It's great to see you, too, McAllery," said Steven, standing over the bed. Now what? Mike had rolled onto his side so that he wouldn't have to look at Steven.

"Well, let's get you up." Steven ripped back the covers. *And* looking *like a person, at least,* he finished to himself. Mike wore a grungy black T-shirt and boxers.

Turning angrily, Mike bit out a curse. Steven ignored him and removed the Walkman from Mike's ears, dodging his clumsy hands.

"Goddammit, Wakefield, get out of here!"

"Get a grip, McAllery," Steven said sharply. He pulled Mike up and shoved some pillows behind his back. Mike managed to get his arms working well enough to hit Steven in the face, a weak, glancing blow that embarrassed both of them.

"You do that one more time and I'll punch you out," Steven warned. That wasn't a line he'd learned from his hospital coaches, but what was he supposed to do? This was different from practicing on the paralyzed patients in the hospital. Most of those people *wanted* to get better, *wanted* to be helped.

"Leave me alone, Wakefield," Mike said coldly.

"Oh, so you can still talk normally," Steven said sarcastically, rummaging for socks in a drawer. "What a relief."

"I didn't ask you to come. But now that you *are* here, I'd be better off if you finished what you started," Mike said flatly.

Steven was startled when he realized what Mike was talking about—Mike wanted to die. The hospital nurses had told Steven that some paralyzed people thought about suicide, especially at first. "Forget it—you're getting dressed," he said, holding up a pair of socks. Mike flopped off the pillows and tried to pull himself away.

"Look, McAllery," Steven said, trying not to show the pity he felt. "I'll be out of your life faster if you just cooperate. Isn't that what you want?"

"I want you to get the hell out of here!" Mike snapped.

"You and me both. Now put on the damn socks and quit being a jerk. Though I know that comes naturally to you."

Angrily Steven grabbed Mike's foot and shoved a sock over his toes. Mike just lay there. Steven tugged at the sock, struggling to get it over Mike's clammy, lifeless foot. Feeling as though he were dressing a large, extremely hateful baby, Steven rolled the sock up and smoothed it out.

Then he picked up the other sock. Mike was staring at the wall, his body twisted, looking completely pathetic.

Why should I bother dressing him when he's only going to lie there all day? Steven wondered. The only reason he could think of was that the judge had sentenced him to help Mike. So he was going to help him, even if they both hated it.

Two hours later, Steven trudged upstairs to his own apartment. He had managed to get both socks on, as well as a clean pair of jeans. Mike's body, still too thin, seemed lost in the jeans that had once been fashionably tight. Then Steven had straightened the covers, opened windows for fresh air, and righted the wheelchair, placing it close at hand. Feeling humiliated, like a servant, he had thrown dirty clothes into the hamper, tidied the living room, and washed dirty dishes.

"This is all stuff you could do for yourself," he had pointed out. "Paralyzed isn't a synonym for pig." Mike had merely grunted, watching him with dislike.

Now he had to go back upstairs, where no doubt he and Billie would argue pointlessly about something. But he guessed he should face her before things got even worse between them.

Maybe she was right. Maybe he had been obsessed with Mike and Jessica's relationship. Probably he had been an idiot to spend so much time staring out the window and worrying about his sister. It's not as though it had even helped—look at the outcome. And he *had* neglected Billie. He'd hardly had time for her or their relationship for almost three months.

Steven pushed open the door and groped for the light switch. The apartment was dark and still. "Billie?" he called. He was answered by silence. "Billie, where are you?"

Chapter Two

"Peter Wilbourne is eating one of those pies for the needy," Elizabeth Wakefield announced later that afternoon, looking through the window of the dorm room.

"You're kidding," Jessica said with a grin, turning around at her desk. "Not generous, lovable Peter. That just can't be true."

"He's choking down the whole thing," Elizabeth said with distaste. "Also, it's clouding up. Looks like rain." Turning around, she popped a tape in the VCR. It was a video of her, reporting for the campus TV station, WSVU. Today was the wrap-up of the secret-society story, and she wanted to make sure she sounded OK as she concluded her feature.

When the cordless phone on Jessica's desk rang, Elizabeth ignored it. Jessica sat bent over a book, a reading lamp shining on her golden hair. Finally, in exasperation, Elizabeth clicked the mute button and grabbed the phone. "Hello?"

"Liz, can we talk?" asked a male voice. "Or are you too busy? It's Todd," he added when she remained silent.

"Well . . ." Elizabeth could feel her face getting warm. She had only seen Todd once in the past few days, and he had been too drunk to see her, luckily. The time before that he had stood in the middle of the campus and shouted for everyone to hear that he would never give her up.

That had been embarrassing and a little scary. Earlier in the year, she had been heartbroken when Todd had dumped her for another girl. But she had another boyfriend now.

"I don't want to bother you," he said. "But I wondered if maybe we could get together and talk about that story . . ." Elizabeth felt instantly guilty. Earlier in the semester, she had uncovered a scandal about preferential treatment some of the star SVU athletes had received. After Todd had gotten busted and suspended from the basketball team for a year, she had promised him that she would do a follow-up story on the university's involvement, but she just hadn't gotten around to it.

She did think the story should be done. After all, the university had offered the athletes the special treatment in the first place. Now it was punishing them for accepting it.

"I'll start on the story soon," she said. "I'll give you a call when I have anything."

"All right," Todd said, not sounding happy. "Talk to you soon, I hope. Bye, Liz."

Elizabeth switched off the phone, then held it in her hand for a minute.

"How's Todd?" Jessica asked, still looking at her book. "Pining away?"

"He's not great," Elizabeth answered, deciding not to mention his drinking. She flopped back on the bed. "How'd you know it was him?"

"Because you're always trying to get rid of him," Jessica said, shrugging.

That made Elizabeth feel even worse. She turned back to the TV and clicked the sound on.

"The students who received academic probation for their role in the secret society must maintain a *B* average or face suspension for the semester," she watched herself say on TV. "Their names will be kept confidential."

"But everybody knows who they are," Elizabeth commented now.

"Try Peter Wilbourne," Jessica mumbled, flicking to the next page of her book. She suddenly turned and looked at Elizabeth. "Is he still dating Celine? Or was Celine dating William White? No, you were dating William White."

Elizabeth winced. The conversation wasn't about her favorite people. As members of the secret society, Celine Boudreaux, her former roommate, William, her former boyfriend, and Peter Wilbourne had almost managed to kill her—literally. William had personally dragged her to a deep pit under the Sigma house and tried to throw her in. Fortunately Tom had rescued her at the last second.

"I haven't seen Celine since she moved out," Elizabeth said. "She's supposed to be working in the cafeteria five days a week as part of her academic probation. Isn't that an incredible concept?" She couldn't help grinning.

"She'll probably wear high heels and full makeup, just to cut up the lettuce," Jessica said, half closing her blue-green eyes. "I can't really see her frumping around in support hose with the rest of the cafeteria ladies."

Elizabeth clicked off the TV.

"Celine was such a witch," Jessica continued. "Ding, dong, the witch is dead." She picked up her blue highlighter again.

"How's the studying going?" Elizabeth asked. It was still strange to see Jessica and a book spending time together.

Jessica shrugged without turning around. "It's going, I guess."

Elizabeth walked over to the window and looked out into the quad. A couple of guys from the Zeta athletic fraternity were mud sliding down the hill on pieces of cardboard. They were all covered in dirt and almost unrecognizable, but Elizabeth could still tell that Todd wasn't among them.

She wondered what Todd would do without sports for a semester. Basketball had been his whole life. *Basketball and me,* she thought. She pushed away the feeling of guilt again. After all, he was the one who had broken up with her. "What are you studying?" she asked her twin.

"Philosophy. I'm pursuing wisdom." Jessica winced. "I could use a little, huh?"

"Look, you're not the only one who's made big mistakes with relationships," Elizabeth said reasonably. "Todd dumped me about five minutes after we got to school. And William White is about the worst person I could have ever picked to go out with."

"Well, he's a nutcase," Jessica said, her face growing serious. "He's in a mental institution now, isn't he?"

Elizabeth shuddered. "Yeah. And I hope I never see him again in my entire life."

Jessica stared down at her desk, her long hair falling around her face. "At least you're recovering from your mistakes. William's gone, you've got Tom—but I'm still married," she said. "I took off my wedding band last night, even though the annulment isn't final." She rubbed

27

her forehead. "I don't *want* to be married. I guess I never did. That's why it's so awful that I ruined Mike's life."

"You didn't ruin his life, Jess," Elizabeth said forcefully. "Nobody *made* Mike buy a gun and go on a rampage with it. Nobody *made* him threaten to hit you or wreck your apartment. He's got to live with what happened."

"So do I," Jessica said sadly.

"So does Steven," Elizabeth said. "Isn't today the day our compassionate older brother has to start helping Mike with his rehabilitation?"

"Yeah." Jessica smiled in spite of herself. "I can't see it, can you? They hate each other."

Elizabeth was relieved to see her sister smile. "Yeah. I'm glad I'm not there to watch," she said, rolling her eyes.

Jessica propped her elbows on her desk and pushed her hands through her hair. "I still hear that shot going off," she said, a tremor in her voice. "I dream about it almost every night."

Elizabeth looked at Jessica with concern. Tears sparkled in her sister's eyes. "I guess you will for a while," Elizabeth said sympathetically.

"Even paralyzed from the waist down, Mike's going to be a handful for Steven," Jessica murmured.

"Jess?" Elizabeth said gently.

"I'm OK with it," Jessica said firmly, but she wouldn't look Elizabeth in the eye.

28

I hope so, Elizabeth thought. "Now that your annulment is almost final and you're living on campus, you can get back in the swing of things," she said in an optimistic voice.

"Yeah, I'm just swingin' with intro to philosophy," Jessica replied sarcastically. "I'm so far behind with all my classes, I'm practically back in last summer."

"You'll catch up," Elizabeth reassured her. "You're smarter at schoolwork than you think, and you've always been able to do anything you really wanted to."

"Yeah, well, thanks." Jessica gave her a half-smile. "At least my mind will be off guys for a while."

"Speaking of guys"—Elizabeth grabbed some books off her desk and hurried to the door—"I have to go meet Tom, but let's have dinner together in the cafeteria. OK?"

"Definitely," Jessica said, uncapping her highlighter again and riffling the pages of her book.

Elizabeth stood half in and half out of the room, swinging the door a little and smiling. She was remembering the expression on Tom's handsome, usually reserved face at lunch today. He had been stalking up and down the cafeteria line, trying to find the exact kind of chef's salad she wanted.

Then she saw that Jessica was staring at her.

"Well, at least we have one fairy-tale ending around here," Jessica said sourly.

"Yeah, I guess we do," Elizabeth answered with a sheepish smile.

What a perfect December day, Tom thought. After the sunny afternoon, it had begun to rain, and now a chill drizzle was splashing against his window. Days like this were great for lying in front of a fire and cuddling under a blanket with the person you loved.

"I love Elizabeth," he told his mirror.

One of his dormmates slammed a cowboy boot into the other side of the wall. Tom knew it was a cowboy boot because Gilbert Simmons, his next-door neighbor, had knocked on the door yesterday and threatened to shove it down his throat if he didn't shut up.

"Give it a *rest,* Watts!" Gilbert yelled.

Tom grinned. Part of him thought he'd lost his mind. But no part of him could blame himself for falling in love with Elizabeth. Whistling, Tom looked in the mirror and stroked back his hair. He looked OK, or at least the way he always did. He opened the door, took the stairs four at a time, and shot out of the dorm into the quad.

He did a Fred Astaire leap along the path. A few umbrellas twisted as people turned to stare at him. *I'm such a dork,* he told himself happily.

Then he noticed Isabella Ricci watching him curiously from the path. She held her books in one hand and twirled a stylish black-and-white umbrella in the other.

"I can't believe I used to think you were re-served," she said, laughing.

Tom smiled, rubbing big teardrops of rain from his face. He was soaking wet, but he didn't care.

"Hey, if you're looking for Danny, he's working out in the gym," Tom said. His room-mate, Danny Wyatt, and Isabella, who was one of Jessica's best friends, had recently started going out.

Isabella nodded, pulling her books under the umbrella. "I'll wait for him in your room. Then when he comes in all sweaty and grimy and ex-hausted, I won't have missed a second of it." Isabella waved good-bye and started down the path.

Smiling, Tom continued on to the TV sta-tion. He controlled his happiness, not doing leaps or exhibiting any other signs of insanity. He didn't want to end up as William White's roommate.

Tom wondered for a second what living in a mental institution was like. He had been in one once while covering a story on homelessness. The inmates had seemed pretty scary, but then, he had visited the dangerous ward. William was probably being coddled and treated like a gentleman somewhere.

Tom had never expected William to actually be committed. It was a spectacular end for a rival. But William deserved his punishment. Grimacing, Tom remembered how he had felt when he'd realized Elizabeth's life was in danger.

Then Tom saw her. Although a light rain was falling, it seemed that the air had never been brighter. Elizabeth hadn't seen him yet—she continued to hurry along the path toward the station.

He loved her so much. He had never, ever loved anyone like this. He knew what he was risking by letting himself be so in love: all living things were fragile, and sometimes they were only with you for a short time.

He caught up with her at the station door.

"Tom!" she said breathlessly, her smile shining like a nearby star. The soft rain beaded in her long hair, turning parts of it dark gold.

He kissed her, with all the need built up from almost three months of holding back his feelings for her. His fingers gently followed the smooth curve of her cheeks. He looked into her sparkling, intelligent eyes, the color of spring leaves and sky.

Elizabeth was trembling, and not just from excitement at seeing him, he suddenly realized. She was wet and cold. Tom managed to pull himself away. "Let's go inside," he said, "and continue this."

Elizabeth nodded. "OK," she said, a dimple appearing in her left cheek. "Drier is better."

Once they were inside the news office, Elizabeth shook some of the rain out of her hair and pointed at a cot in the corner. "That's new."

"Um, yeah."

Does she think I got that to try to lure her into sleeping with me? he wondered. "I bought it for late nights. And for when . . . Isabella is in the room with Danny. *Or did I really buy the cot just in case?* Tom felt himself turning red.

Elizabeth's laugh was like the sun coming out. "I've never seen you blush before," she said.

"I'm not," Tom replied, trying to steady his voice. He dragged his eyes away from the cot. "It's just—"

"You don't have to feel like you're tattling on your roommate," she said, flicking on the computer. "Let's talk about work."

Tom frowned. He would have preferred to get back to their kiss.

"I told Todd we'd get started on that story about the university's involvement in the athletics scandal," Elizabeth continued, rapidly clicking keys.

Tom threw himself into his desk chair and looked at her. "I don't think that's such a hot topic anymore," he said, although he knew he didn't really want to do the story because it would involve Todd Wilkins. "What about writing up the Bruce Patman story?" he asked. "He just got a ten-million-dollar trust fund dumped in his lap."

Elizabeth made a face. "I don't think anything to do with Bruce 'The Ego' Patman is such a hot topic," she said.

Tom put his hand on her arm, then moved it up to the soft skin on the back of her neck. She smiled and leaned against him as he put his arms around her.

"I don't know what story we should do," she murmured, touching her lips to his shoulder.

Tom turned her face toward his, and they kissed. No matter how many times he kissed her, it still felt inexpressibly new and wonderful. Every kiss seemed to make time stop.

Elizabeth shifted over to sit in his lap, knocking a book off the desk. "Oops," she said, reaching down to retrieve it. "Look, it's Elizabeth Barrett Browning. I think she's trying to remind me that I have to plan a poetry reading for my lit class."

Tom picked up her hand and kissed it. "I have a better idea. Let's plan something for our one-week anniversary. It's next Saturday."

"A whole week," Elizabeth said, smiling. "It's still hard to believe we're together, isn't it?"

Tom looked at her for a moment, his face

growing thoughtful. "Sometimes I can't believe it at all," he said softly.

"Should we go out for dinner?" she suggested.

"Yeah. But not to some stuffy, overpriced place like Da Vinci's, where every dumb jock goes to celebrate a completed pass," he said firmly, touching the silken tips of her hair. "Let's find a special place of our own."

"Uh . . . yeah, that sounds good." Elizabeth didn't meet his eyes.

"What?" he asked, feeling a jolt of alarm. What did that lukewarm response mean? Did she only want to see him around the station? Did she not care enough about him to celebrate being together? Or did she just think he had lousy ideas?

"Nothing." She looked at him and smiled wryly. "It's just that talking about jocks reminded me of Todd. I really do have to start on that story for him. He called today."

"What did he want?" Tom asked, trying to keep the irritation out of his voice. He was sick of Todd. Todd was constantly calling Elizabeth, worrying her, trying to push his way back into her life.

"He just wanted to talk." Elizabeth shrugged slightly.

"I'll bet. He hasn't made much of a secret of what he wants to talk about."

Elizabeth sighed. "It's over between Todd

and me," she said. "I'm not interested in being his girlfriend anymore. But I feel like I owe it to him to help him out. We were such . . . good friends once. I've known him my whole life. I can't pretend he doesn't exist."

Tom's stomach turned and he looked away. He hated it when she talked about her old romance with Todd. He knew it was wrong of him, but he was jealous of all those years when Todd had taken her to football games and out for ice cream, done homework with her in the kitchen, and parked at makeout spots and kissed her.

"Stop." Elizabeth touched her lips to his forehead. "I'm only going to talk to him about the sports story. Todd's an old friend, and he's miserable."

Tom started to say that Todd's misery was his own problem. Was he supposed to feel sorry for some fool who had ditched her and then regretted it?

But Elizabeth put a not-too-gentle hand over his mouth. Then she pulled it away and pressed her lips to his, exquisite and soft as a petal, and he forgot that his life had ever been anything but the sound of December rain on the roof and his love in his arms.

He caught her hair, smoothing back the damp gold strands. Then he moved his hands down her back, holding her closer. For several moments she stayed locked in his embrace and the passion of their deep, lingering kiss. Then she moved away so that she could look at him again.

"Let's be careful with each other," she whispered.

After a moment Tom nodded. He closed his eyes and waited for his breathing to slow.

Elizabeth stood and interlaced her fingers with his. "I think we'd better head to the cafeteria before it closes," she said. "We still have to eat, right?"

"Let's try out the cot for just a minute first," Tom said.

The mop fell over, whacking Celine sharply on the shin. Muttering curses, Celine backed it up against the wall again. The mop slopped and slurped in the bucket and dumped cold, dirty water on her tennis shoe.

"If it's the last thing I do, and it may well be the last, because the good Lord did not intend my body for such treatment, I will get Elizabeth Wakefield for this," Celine muttered.

No one heard her. In the cafeteria kitchen, far behind the food lines and any form of civilization, Celine had absolutely no company. Unless she counted the two overweight women in hairnets who were frying burgers and stirring vats of mystery stew.

Just the fact that Celine had to mash her thick, naturally curly blond mane under a hairnet for five entire breakfasts, lunches, and dinners a week was enough to make her want to see Elizabeth Wakefield slowly turning on a spit over a fire.

Celine thought a lot about getting even with Elizabeth. Better to think about revenge than about the rest of her own life.

First there was the cafeteria work, which was so horrible it could only be a nightmare that she could hope to wake up from someday. Then, after work, she spent her free time in her depressing little room off campus. One of her next-door neighbors was a short, dorky guy with Coke-bottle glasses who ran off at four every morning to check on the white mice and fruit flies in his science experiments. Her other neighbor played saxophone in the school jazz band and wailed the blues at the most unsettling moments, like when she was trying to apply mascara or pluck her eyebrows.

"What to do," Celine muttered, looking darkly at the shortest and squattest of her co-workers, who had just flung a basket of onion rings into the deep-fat fryer. "Hmm. If I could just make *Elizabeth* ugly again."

To Celine's delight, Elizabeth had gotten a rocky start at the beginning of the semester, especially after Todd dumped her. She had drowned her misery in Twinkies, Ding Dongs, and Ho-Hos, and had gained a hefty twenty pounds. Celine had helped make the problem worse by putting boxes of chocolate, bags of chips, and other goodies everywhere possible in the room they shared. But unfortunately, Elizabeth had since lost all the weight and, awful as it was to admit, looked more beautiful than ever.

"If only there was a fat pill I could stick in her food that would turn her into a whale," Celine continued, even though she couldn't hear herself over the thump and spray of the giant cafeteria dishwasher. "How *can* I get even with that girl?"

The dishwasher clanked and shook, then fell silent. Celine looked at it, struck for a moment by the possibility of luring Elizabeth into the kitchen and then running her through the pots and pans cycle.

"Ms. Perfect's goldilocks would sure take a beating in there," Celine remarked, drawing closer. "Those jet sprays would give her a guaranteed six-week perm."

The dishwasher vibrated, lurched, and suddenly sprang into life. It tossed a curtain of sizzling water and mist straight at Celine.

She dodged most of it. "I will not bend," she said through gritted teeth, wiping suds and makeup from her cheek. "I'll be like the South at the Battle of Bull Run." The South *had* won that battle, hadn't it?

Celine furiously whipped the mop's lank strands into a corner. She couldn't transfer out of this school any more than she could transfer out of the kitchen from hell: no other school would accept her with the black blotch she had on her record.

"I wasn't even *in* the stupid secret society," she said to herself irritably. "I was just in the wrong place at the wrong time."

All right, a couple of wrong places, a couple of wrong times. She had been dating Peter Wilbourne, and trying to date William White, when she had found out they were both members of that moronic society. The night of the bust she'd actually called Tom from the underground chambers of Sigma house to try to save Miss Priss. Didn't that count for anything?

"That's the last time I'll ever do a good deed," Celine muttered, dumping half a bottle of pink floor-cleaning acid into the bucket. "People who are stupid enough to do good deeds instead of watching out for their own skin wind up in jail." Because of Elizabeth, Celine had spent eleven hours in a jail cell full of stinking, cynical women who had snatched her cigarettes and played with her hair. The authorities had taken their sweet time about tracking down her father in Copenhagen to wire bail money.

Well, at least *she* was out of jail. Where was William now?

Chapter
Three

"Lila isn't just cool," Jessica said, that evening at dinnertime, as she carefully sorted postcards from Lila into piles from Genoa, Rome, and Venice. "She's beyond cool. She doesn't even have to try anymore." Jessica was beginning to enjoy her conversation with herself. "Lila's actually been to the beach on the Italian Riviera."

Jessica was talking to herself because Elizabeth—steady, trustworthy, Old Faithful Elizabeth—had apparently forgotten that she and Jessica had a dinner date. Being blown off by her twin was a new experience for Jessica, and she didn't like it much.

"But I guess I can understand being in love," Jessica said, trying to feel generous as she wiped away a tear. "I just wonder where Liz is going with this." Unlike Jessica herself, who had been in love with at least twenty guys, although only one, *truly*, Elizabeth had never been in love before.

41

"Unless you count Todd," Jessica muttered, turning over a postcard showing gaily striped gondolas in Venice. "But that relationship was about as exciting as a spinach milk shake." Jessica didn't think love, Elizabeth-style, was the real thing. Elizabeth's dates with Todd had been racy adventures like holding hands under a beach umbrella or having a spirited game of miniature golf. Then—killer moment!—a peck on the lips at the doorstep.

Jessica shook her head to clear it. She had gotten tired of studying about an hour ago. Certainly her neck had gotten tired. Bookworms apparently had muscles she hadn't developed yet.

She put down the postcards. She'd go to dinner by herself. This was another first in her life, and she wasn't looking forward to it. On the way out the door she grabbed her chemistry book from the desk. *Am I turning into a nerd?* she thought. *I wonder how you know for sure.*

In the cafeteria, Jessica walked slowly toward the food line, trying to look very interested in the choices for the main course. Between the stainless-steel shelves holding sandwiches, fruit, and cookies, she caught a glimpse of a strange figure in a tight orange dress, swishing a mop and wearing a hairnet.

"Celine?" she called, grinning.

Celine froze in mid-mop and glared at Jessica for a long moment. Then she smiled sweetly.

"Well, if it isn't Little Miss Trouble," she said. "Anybody shoot it out to the death over you today?"

"Not yet," Jessica answered, tossing her hair. "But it's only six thirty."

"And how's Elizabeth, Patron Saint of Pillness?" Celine smirked and leaned on her mop.

"Well, she's not working in the cafeteria, at least," Jessica said innocently, plucking a bottle of apple juice out of the crushed ice and setting it on her tray. "How *is* life among the dishwashers?"

"One more word, honey, and you're going to be wearing this mop," Celine said, shaking it. "Don't worry about me. A Boudreaux will always come out on top."

"Yeah. You might make head janitor if you work at it," Jessica said, laughing. "See you around, Celine."

Jessica pushed her tray along the food line, hoping she could find someone to eat with. To her relief, she spotted Isabella in the line over by the napkins. Then she noticed several other Thetas with her.

Jessica started to turn away. These days, the Thetas made it clear that she was a nonperson. It was a major switch from Jessica's first few weeks at SVU—the sorority had practically begged her to join. Back then, Jessica had been a golden girl with just the right Theta image. She was also a legacy of her mother, the famous

Alice Wakefield, who had made Theta Alpha Theta *the* sorority on campus.

Jessica sighed as she headed for an empty table in a corner. Now every single Theta remembered only her marriage to Mike, and the shooting. When Jessica ran into any of the sisters on campus, they sneered or looked right through her.

Except for Isabella.

"Jess!" Isabella called, setting her tray on a nearby table. "Come on over and eat with us."

Jessica hesitated a moment. The Thetas might start in on her again. But it was just possible they were ready to bury the hatchet. Either way, eating alone would be worse. *It's not like I have better plans,* Jessica thought, heading toward Isabella.

Halfway across the world, Lila dug her toes into the smooth white sand of the beach and looked out to sea. Tisiano was jet-skiing about a hundred yards offshore. The motor roared above the slap of the waves. Lila could hear bits of song from a nearby radio that belonged to some of the other chic people visiting this gorgeous beach on the Italian Riviera.

"No more business today," she said softly to herself. "Just as soon as you work off that tension from your meeting, you'll be with me all night."

The nights when he was gone were always the worst. Lila missed the warmth of his arms around her, the softness of his lips on her body, his quiet words of love. When she was alone, listening to the rustle of the unfamiliar Italian trees outside her window and the calls of strange night birds, Lila felt homesick for her family and friends and for California.

As she watched the green waters of the Mediterranean, Tisiano waved, then expertly jumped the Jet Ski over some rough water. When he had stopped bouncing, he smiled at her and zoomed on.

Lila sighed and brushed some dry sand off her leg. She had stopped worrying about Tisiano—there was no point. She had gotten used to flying upside down with him in their orange-and-red plane, to his drag racing any other Ferrari or Porsche he met on the road, and to his occasional business dealings with computer salespeople who were also mafiosi. He always came back to her. And the truth was that she loved his wild streak—it matched or even outdid her own.

It's just that I care about him so much, she thought, heaping wet sand into a red plastic bucket. She carried the bucket a safe distance from the incoming tide and turned it over. She would make a sand castle, looking just like the one in Spain that Tisiano talked about building.

45

She would make it with lots of turrets and gardens, and a moat.

Lila looked out at the water again. Tisiano was closer to shore now, about fifty yards out. But this time she saw a thin line of blue flame licking along the Jet Ski. That couldn't be—the glare of the setting sun on the water was making her see things. . . .

The explosion rocked the air, hurling bolts of sound across the waves to shake the beach. Lila fell to the ground, partly from concussion and partly from shock. A ball of flame leaped to the sky and raged briefly. Then the sea was calm and green and silent again, only small waves disturbing its glassy surface.

There was no Jet Ski.

There was no Tisiano.

"It's an important meeting," Bryan Nelson said to Nina Harper. He stopped eating to look at her closely. "Are you sure you can't make it?"

"It's an important physics test," Nina countered. "Deriving the Lorenz equation will be on it, and it'll take me most of the night to figure it out."

Bryan frowned slightly, then leaned over until his dark, handsome face was just inches from hers. "Nina," he said patiently, "I must not be putting this strongly enough or you would understand. The Black Students Union meeting isn't just important. It's critical. We're going to vote on actions to combat racism on campus and keep the black students safe. We were both put in the hospital by that racist crap. You have to be at the meeting. What kind of signal is it going to send if you don't show? It's like you don't care."

"I do care," Nina insisted. She realized that she was quickly gobbling the food on her tray just to have something to do besides meet Bryan's hazel eyes. She could feel them drilling into her. "Oh, look, there's Elizabeth!" she said with relief. "Another diet success story."

Elizabeth walked into the cafeteria hand in hand with Tom, smiling up at him. Nina waved, then waved again. Finally Elizabeth saw her and waved back. Nina started to motion her over before she noticed that Bryan was leaving.

"So what's it going to be?" he asked, crumpling his napkin and tossing it on his tray.

"Bryan—" Nina took a deep breath. "I'm caught here. I *have* to do well on this physics test. I have to. I'll be at the meeting if I possibly can." She smiled tentatively at him. Maybe that would do it. She didn't want to lose him. Already they'd had such an incredible time together, exploring politics, economics, and social issues together. They had laughed over their different backgrounds—Nina's parents were the most conservative businesspeople in America,

47

while Bryan was the son of sixties-style radicals.

It seemed incredible that he would drop her over missing one meeting.

But he didn't return her smile. "You aren't much of an activist, are you?" he said, getting up from the table. "Like you told me, I guess I'll see you tonight if I see you."

Elizabeth leaned a little against Tom in the food line. Out of habit she took a bowl of cottage cheese, a peach to slice on it, and a small, wilted green salad, but for once caloric intake was the last thing on her mind.

Out of the corner of her eye Elizabeth saw a strange, almost glowing orange shape back in the kitchen. It vaguely crossed her mind that the food attendants must have new uniforms that would make them visible in the dark.

Then Tom kissed her, and Elizabeth stopped seeing anything at all.

"Where should we sit?" he asked her. A guy behind them had been nudging Tom with his tray, trying to move them along.

"How about over there?" Elizabeth asked, pointing to a completely empty table. She had seen Nina and Bryan, but they seemed to be having some kind of heavy conversation, and the next minute they'd left—Bryan ten paces ahead of Nina and gaining.

"Lead on," Tom said.

I hope Nina doesn't have trouble in her paradise, Elizabeth thought, raising her tray high over the heads of other people to get to her table. *I'll track her down in the library later and find out what's wrong.* Nina was usually easy to find—she practically lived in the all-night reading room.

As she set down her tray, Elizabeth noticed Alexandra Rollins, formerly Enid Rollins and formerly her best friend, eating with Todd at a table nearby. It was still hard to believe she and Enid weren't friends anymore.

"Alex and I were best friends and now we don't even say hi to each other," she murmured to Tom.

"That was before she became a jock groupie," Tom said, lifting plates from the tray and shoving it to the far end of the table.

"And before the whole sports scandal," she said. Alex was furious with Elizabeth for that. Her boyfriend, Mark Gathers, had gotten busted, and then he'd left SVU for good. Alex blamed Elizabeth.

Tom shrugged. "A lot of people are mad at you for doing that story. Mostly people who did something wrong." He looked meaningfully over at Todd, who stared coldly back.

"I know." Elizabeth still didn't like seeing Alex's angry, unhappy expression whenever they ran into each other.

Elizabeth had barely begun to eat her salad when she heard Todd's voice behind her. "Can I borrow your ketchup?"

"Borrow one from another table," Tom said irritably. "Can't you do better than that?"

"No, I can't," Todd retorted. "I really want your ketchup."

"Can we stop this?" Elizabeth asked incredulously. She handed Todd the bottle of ketchup.

"Thank you, Elizabeth," Todd said stiffly. He returned to Alex and sat down. Elizabeth could still feel his eyes on her.

Tom's expression was angry.

"Let's not lose it over ketchup," Elizabeth said.

Tom let out a breath. "Yeah. You're right. OK."

Elizabeth suddenly spotted Jessica, sitting with Isabella and the other Thetas. "Oh, no!" she cried. "I can't believe it! I completely forgot I was supposed to meet Jessica for dinner."

"She's got company," Tom said, digging into his burger.

Elizabeth hesitated.

"Don't worry about her," he said. "She's enjoying herself. She's where she belongs."

Elizabeth looked at the Theta table. Jessica was laughing, tossing her golden hair as she pointed a saltshaker at Isabella. "I guess you're right," Elizabeth said.

*   *   *

Todd watched Elizabeth finish her salad and begin on her cottage cheese. He spun the ketchup bottle on its side.

"Stop it," Alex said wearily. "You'll make yourself sick. Believe me, I know."

"Stop what?" Todd asked, giving the ketchup another twist. "This is fun—try it." He flipped the bottle to her, and Alex caught it.

"Stop staring at Elizabeth. You don't have to pretend with me." Alex raised compassionate, teary eyes to his and replaced the ketchup in the middle of the table. "We know each other's secrets."

"Like what?" Todd asked. The ketchup rolled off the other side of the table. He crawled underneath Alex's chair to retrieve it.

"Like that we've both been deserted!" Alex muttered, looking down. She could only see the soles of Todd's shoes. "I don't even know if Mark's ever coming back from that stupid basketball tryout in L.A. He doesn't care enough to tell me!"

"Well, I'm one up on you, then," Todd said heavily, reemerging with the ketchup and a stray spoon. "Because I know I've lost Elizabeth. But anyway, Mark won't be back if he makes that semipro team. You probably should count him out of your life."

Alex hung her head. She felt like crying, but she wasn't quite pathetic enough to start bawling in the cafeteria while the whole school watched. Besides, she was saving several weeks' worth of tears for the day she knew for sure that Mark, and any chance for glamour and happiness in her life, were gone for good.

Alex and Todd watched Elizabeth and Tom in silence.

They were smiling at each other, talking quietly as they ate.

Todd groaned. "I can't stand any more of this," he said, rising. "I'm going back to my room to study. If I flunk out, I'll really have hit bottom. It's not like I can do anything to get Elizabeth back. Elizabeth has changed—we're on separate tracks now. I just have to accept that, and admire her for what she is. From afar."

"I'm not so sure she's changed," Alex said. "I mean, *we* sort of did, but now we're changing back." *In my case to good old Enid Rollins, dweeb fatale of Sweet Valley High,* she thought. *God, I'm really depressing myself.* "So anyway, maybe what came between you two is gone now," Alex said.

Todd looked over at Elizabeth. She and Tom had finished eating and were getting up from their table. Tom kissed Elizabeth and grabbed her hand as they headed for the door.

"No," Todd said. "It's still there."

"I've never looked good in plaids," Jessica confessed. In the cat-eat-cat world of the

52

Thetas, admitting a beauty flaw was a sign of submission.

Magda threw her an approving look. "Your colors are more solid and cool, I'd think," she said.

"Can't beat a blonde in aquamarine," Jessica said breezily. *I'm doing all right,* she thought. *I sound almost like I used to. The Thetas seem to think so too.*

She had come close to disaster. When she'd sat down next to Isabella, the table conversation had died as though somebody pulled the plug. When Jessica had finally dared to look up, every gaze was on her: some accusing, some curious, some disdainful.

"I think the rain's stopping!" Isabella said brightly at last. "Thank God—I can start taming my hair again."

"You have gorgeous hair and you know it," Kimberly Schyler told her, not sounding completely kind. "I need humidity to even wake my hair up to a frizz."

"I might get my hair cut in a bob," Jessica said before someone else could break in. "You know, short, sleek, with the sides swishing across my face when I turn my head."

"I don't know if that would work for you," said Denise Waters, cupping her own lovely face in her hand.

"Your hair's a sensational color, Jess." Isabella

touched a strand. "I'd say the more you have of it, the better."

It's working, Jessica thought. *They're opening up and accepting me. Thank you, Isabella. Someday I really will do you a big favor to pay you back for this.*

The conversation went on swimmingly. Jessica could feel her face relax, her remarks become funnier and more natural. Then she saw Isabella glance sharply toward the food line. Jessica followed her wary gaze.

Alison Quinn had just put a Diet Coke on her tray and was turning, headed for the Theta table. About halfway there she saw Jessica and froze in midstep. Then she arranged her pink-glossed lips into something that passed for a smile and marched over to join them. She plunked down in the empty chair next to Jessica, apparently not seeing her at all, and put her napkin in her lap.

The table was absolutely still as the sorority sisters held their collective breath. Jessica could feel a flush starting on her neck. She wanted to whip out a remark to prove that Alison wasn't intimidating her, but she didn't dare break the thick, icy silence.

Suddenly Alison turned and jumped in apparent astonishment at discovering who was sitting next to her.

"Jessica!" she cried. "Poor, poor Jessica. Out

54

of mourning clothes already? Oh no; I'm sorry. Of course, you wouldn't be in black. Your husband's not dead—just crippled for life, right?"

Jessica bit her lip. The faces of Alison Quinn and the other Thetas started to blur around the edges.

"Yes, he's crippled," she said, scrambling out of her chair and grabbing her tray and tote. "Would you excuse me? I have a lot of studying to do."

"Jessica, don't go," Isabella said, looking concerned. "We don't have to talk about Mike."

There it was, out in the open. The subject she had wanted everyone to forget.

"I really have to get some work done, Iz," Jessica said. "Thanks anyway."

"Don't burn yourself out," Denise called sympathetically.

Jessica hurried out of the cafeteria, away from Alison Quinn's cruelty, the interested stares of the other girls, and, hardest to bear, the look of pity on the faces of Isabella and Denise.

No, we don't have to talk about Mike, Jessica thought as the wet wind swirling outside stung the hot tears on her cheeks. *But I've got to think about him forever.*

Chapter
Four

On Sunday night Denise Waters popped a french fry into her mouth and gazed for a minute at the other students eating and talking in the coffeehouse. Then she went back to reading her sociology book. "Want a fry, Win?" she offered.

When he didn't say anything, Denise looked up. "Fry?" she asked. "Fry fry?"

She's looking at Bruce Patman, Winston Egbert thought, feeling sick. *Macho, self-confident, rich Bruce Patman, president of the Sigmas. I've been going out with her for only a week and already I'm losing her. Probably Denise goes out with me only because she wants to study how a single man can live in an all-female dorm without losing his identity.*

"Hello, Winnie?" Denise said. "You're sitting with me. You're looking at me. But you seem to be having an out-of-body experience."

"Denise, admit it," Winston burst out. "You only hang out with me because I'm neurotic. I'm a case study. You want to write your doctorate in sociology on me."

"That makes you pretty important," Denise said, her clear blue eyes sparkling with laughter. "But actually I'm going out with you because you're sweet, sensitive, and completely weird."

"Gee, thanks," Winston said. "I think." He could spend a couple of hours in his room tonight trying to figure out if Denise had just complimented him or insulted him.

"Win, my best friend!" Bruce Patman boomed, clapping Winston on the shoulder. "Sitting with my prettiest friend," he continued, swinging around a chair from another table to sit next to Denise. "How do you do it, Denise? How can someone as smart as you be the best-looking girl on campus?"

"You're in a good mood," Denise observed. Winston felt what seemed to be pointy teeth chewing on his liver.

"I've got reason to be. I just got back from shopping for some ski clothes and a new four-wheel-drive. I bought a fire-engine-red Jeep Cherokee Limited, loaded with extras—Sony CD player, leather seats, ski rack, the works. It's unbelievable." Bruce snapped his fingers. "I want to ski Aspen this winter."

"Playing with the rich and famous?" Winston asked snidely.

Bruce winked. "You bet. I guess you heard my good news—I won't be hurting for money anytime soon."

"I love to ski," Denise said. "I tried Taos last year over winter break. Do you ski, Winnie?"

"I have enough trouble not tripping over my feet, just the way they are," Winston said. "I can imagine what would happen to me if they were six feet longer."

Bruce laughed uproariously. Denise gave a one-sided Mona Lisa smile. Winston felt the tips of his ears turn red.

Just shut up, he told himself. *There's really no need for you to speak. Just sit here quietly and hate Bruce because he's rich, doesn't make people laugh when he talks, and is about to steal Denise away to Aspen without even really trying.*

"Winston's quite a guy," Bruce said, chuckling. "Has been ever since high school. Remember the time you spewed chili down the front of Amanda Gray's dress, Win? I bet that's a memory she'll cherish forever."

Winston cleared his throat and attempted to look dignified.

"Listen, I've got to take off and finish my shopping list, but don't forget you owe me a date this week, Denise." Bruce wagged a finger at her.

"Date?" Winston squeaked, forgetting his vow of silence. He didn't need this on top of the Amanda Gray story. He was already thinking about accidentally "spewing" the coffee left in his cup onto Bruce's new, expensive ski sweater.

"Yep. I'll call you tonight." Bruce winked again and pushed back his chair. "See ya."

Winston watched Bruce's muscular, long-legged strides and the authoritative way he smacked open the coffeehouse door.

"He's Mr. Moneybags all of a sudden," Denise commented, apparently not noticing that Winston was turning several shades of green. "It must be wild to suddenly get control of a trust fund worth a couple million. I heard he bought a Cessna."

Winston bit what was left of his fingernails. He had lost Denise, whether she knew it or not. How could a nonskiing clown compete with a rich god in a Cessna?

"Denise—" Winston choked. He couldn't go on. He loved her. With every single thought. With every last breath he had. But why should she stay with him? He couldn't think of a single reason. Winston dropped his head on the table.

Denise finally seemed to notice that she was killing him. "Win, Bruce and I are working on a sociology project together. It's not a date."

"Promise?" Winston asked. He could feel

himself dissolving into the soft blue of her eyes, into that heavenly smile.

"Of course." Denise went back to watching the crowd.

"Will you tell me why I'm weird?" Winston asked wistfully.

Denise laughed and kissed his nose. "That's going to take a *really* long time. Why don't I tell you later, in the complete privacy of my room?"

"OK," Winston said. As a matter of fact, that was much more than OK.

He wasn't OK, though. Denise would be alone with Bruce for an entire evening. At Sigma house, where the brothers kept scorecards on the physical charms of the women they had over. Sigma house was the animal house.

Of course, Denise would never be a part of any of that.

But Winston couldn't help imagining Bruce kissing her. And the thought was enough to demolish him.

The California sun turned Jessica's hair into a shower of gold as she and Isabella walked across campus on Monday morning. Jessica was glad the sun was shining. Her life was gloomy enough without clouds blotting the sky.

"Danny and I are going to try a new café in town before class," Isabella said. "They have yummy scones and forty varieties of tea."

"Sounds like fun," Jessica said with a sigh. Her own plans weren't a very good topic for conversation. She was going to visit Mike. Another day to have the exact opposite of fun, on top of yesterday's disaster with the Thetas. "Dinner yesterday was terrible," she said glumly.

"Yeah," Isabella agreed. "But actually Alison could have been a lot worse." Isabella stopped, handed Jessica her books, and gathered her dark hair in a tortoiseshell clip. She frowned. "I don't know if you can ever become a Theta now, Jess. I mean, look at your social track record at SVU. First you moved in with and married Mike McAllery, who, to put it politely, is a nightmare. Now you're trying to get the marriage annulled. Not exactly a dream life for a society girl. You snubbed the whole sorority by missing socials and other pledge events. Then, when you were wearing that cute little apron and waiting on tables at the coffeehouse, you told Alison Quinn, vice president of the Thetas, to up hers. Come *on*."

"At least things can't get worse," Jessica said, with a cheeriness she didn't feel. She handed Isabella back her books. "Who said I wanted to repledge?" she asked.

"Well, *if* you do, I've thought about what your chances are." Isabella frowned. "They're not hopeless, despite everything you've done.

Your mother is still a Theta legend, and you're a legacy. There's also me."

"I know you've always been on my side," Jessica said seriously.

"I think I can give you some real help. I'll probably be vice president of the Thetas next year. Alison will be president—she'll be a senior, and she's got the money and connections. She won't be the kind of Theta president your mother was, but she's got a lot of support in the sorority. People like it that she's rich and wants to make the sorority very exclusive. The Thetas who support me care about other things—outreach work, members' characters."

Isabella looked off into space. "Getting you into the Thetas could turn into a real power struggle," she murmured.

"I don't even know if I really want to join," Jessica said honestly. "Do you want to eat together tonight? We could talk about it then."

"I've got a Theta dinner." Suddenly Isabella smiled. "There he is. Danny!" she called.

Jessica's mouth turned down. "And there's Alison," she muttered. Alison and Danny had both appeared around the journalism building at the same time, but Alison was walking very slowly. Danny seemed to be waiting for her, then he shrugged and picked up his pace.

She doesn't want to be seen with Danny because

he's black, Jessica thought. *What a prejudiced little witch*.

Danny jogged up to Isabella and hugged her tight. "What's your morning been like?" he asked.

"It just got much better," Isabella said, so obviously sincere that she didn't even sound corny. Isabella's face was glowing as Danny's lips touched hers in a good-morning kiss.

Jessica tried not to look envious. She almost wished Danny and Isabella weren't so happy together. Seeing them made her head thump with tired advice: she should have gone out with someone her own age, she should have found someone with the same interests, she should have listened when people who cared about her told her to stay away from Mike.

Alison stopped in front of Jessica and looked her over without saying a word. "Good morning, ladies," she said coldly. "I just remembered someone *important* I have to see. Talk to you later, Isabella."

"At dinner," Isabella mumbled.

Jessica started to walk away.

"Jess!" Isabella called, sounding guilty. "Where are you going?"

"Just, uh, for a walk. Have fun, you guys," she said, barely meaning it.

"You too," Danny replied automatically.

Oh, yeah, a blast, Jessica thought as turned

64

left on the path and trudged around puddles left from yesterday's rain.

Jessica stopped in the middle of the parking lot. "I don't have to go there," she said out loud. If she didn't see Mike, though, guilt would follow her everywhere, like a black bird flapping its wings over the sun.

She climbed in her red Kharmann Ghia and sat. *I could just go for a drive.*

"Attempted murder," the lawyer said, leaning back in his chair. "You could do real jail time. A jury would take one look at that pretty blond girl you tried to kill and convict you on the spot."

William White stared stonily at the wall. He hadn't said a word the entire twenty minutes he had been in this office, nor did he intend to say one.

Neither, it seemed, did his parents. His father sat as frozen as William. His mother's mouth curved down in a disgusted grimace.

I'll bet you could use a martini, William thought. *So could I.* These entire proceedings— his arrest, the hours in jail before his parents posted bond, his future jail sentence—seemed unreal. How could such utter fools possibly judge *him*?

The lawyer, Mr. Carson, didn't seem to mind talking to himself. "The only other possible pleas are guilty but insane, and incompetent to stand trial by reason of insanity," he continued. "I recommend the second."

William's mother shrugged slightly.

"Your parents and I have discussed this. They want to avoid the embarrassment of a criminal trial. They also don't want you to go to jail," Mr. Carson said to William. "So they're committing you to the Harrington Institution."

"Where you can recover from your difficult time at school," Mrs. White announced.

William narrowed his eyes.

"It's a mental institution, but a gentleman's one," Mr. Carson continued. "You'll be treated relatively well, I think. Certainly better than you would be in jail. But there's always one catch with an insanity plea: You won't be released until the staff doctors certify you're sane. To convince them of that you'll have to toe the line—their line. They might decide you're sane tomorrow, or they might wait until you're seventy."

The lawyer's voice droned on without William hearing it. All he heard was Elizabeth's clear voice, reciting poetry. *"When we two parted/In silence and tears,/Half broken-hearted/To sever for years . . ."* Byron. She must miss William. Despite what had happened. She had admired him so much.

He still loved her. He knew she hadn't meant for him to be sent away. In her journalistic frenzy, she hadn't tried to understand the secret society. It was a society of elites, and she was definitely a member.

He would explain it to her through poetry, through wine. And if she still couldn't see and she had to die, she would be just as lovely dead. Like a Greek marble statue, an ode to perfection.

William frowned. The idea of shoving her in the pit had been crude. He'd let Wilbourne rush him.

"Well," Mr. Carson said, pushing back from his massive desk and standing, "I'm sorry it's come to this. I've been your attorney for twenty years, Glen, and the worst legal problem we've had to deal with was—"

"Thank you for your time," Mr. White said smoothly, gliding to the desk with his hand out-stretched.

"Pale grew thy cheek and cold,/Colder thy kiss;/Truly that hour foretold sorrow to this," William thought. He smiled.

Tom's chair creaked. It was Monday afternoon, and he and Elizabeth were studying in her room. Elizabeth turned a page of the collected works of Elizabeth Barrett Browning and looked over. No, he was still studying. He hadn't done that to distract her. She returned to her book, which she had already read during high school. Maybe that was why it was boring her now. She wanted to sit in Tom's lap and talk to him.

Tom cleared his throat. *Time for a scientific experiment,* Elizabeth thought. *Let's clock the time until he turns a page.*

One minute passed. Two. *He isn't turning pages.*

Elizabeth could feel a silly grin start on her face. *Stop it,* she scolded herself. *Or I'll make you try out for cheerleading. Don't watch him. Even if you can't keep your mind on your work, don't look over there.*

Her eyes moved to the bed. When she forced herself to look up, Tom was staring at the same thing. They caught each other.

"Study break," he said. "One very small kiss."

He walked over to her desk and pulled her up out of her chair. She kissed him lightly. A shiver ran from her neck to her knees. He pressed his body against hers and gently worked his hand under her sweater. It was cool on her warm stomach.

This feels so unbelievable, Elizabeth thought. When she and Todd had made out, she had thought her physical feelings were powerful, but they were nothing like this. Hot desire swept through her. Her head spun until she thought she might faint. She fell backward onto the bed, with Tom on top of her.

The phone rang loudly.

They both pulled back their hands, Tom from under her sweater, Elizabeth from under his shirt. Elizabeth slowly sat up, pushing her hair out of her eyes.

Tom sat up, leaned his elbows on his knees, and dropped his head into his hands.

"Let it ring," he muttered.

"It might be important," Elizabeth said. "With everything that's happened to Jessica and Steven—"

"OK, answer it," Tom said with a groan. He put his head under the pillow.

Elizabeth cautiously picked up the phone. "Hello?"

"Liz? Hi, it's Todd. I wondered if you had a few minutes to talk about that story," he said.

Elizabeth could tell he was trying not to sound impatient. There was something else in his voice too. Loneliness? Fear? She wasn't sure.

She didn't know what to say. She hadn't even thought about the story since the last time he'd called.

"I wouldn't ask you for a favor if it wasn't important," Todd said. "Can't you find a little time for me?"

"Not right now," Elizabeth said, looking at her pillow. Tom emerged from underneath it and glared at her.

"Is *he* there?" Todd asked suddenly.

"Listen, Todd. I'm sorry, but I've got to go."

When Tom heard the name, he sat up quickly and reached for the phone.

"I'll talk to you later," Elizabeth said, dodging Tom's hands. "I promise I'll get going on the story. OK? Bye."

She hung up before Todd could object. "Don't interrupt my calls," she said sternly to Tom.

"Why not? That one was a waste of time," Tom said, his dark eyes smoldering.

"Well, at least it made us stop. We were going too fast." Elizabeth sat at her desk again.

"Yeah, I know. It's just so easy to keep going—"

"But we can't." Sometimes it scared Elizabeth how they could start kissing, and keep on kissing, and usually most of the night disappeared. At this rate she might wake up on graduation day having done nothing but made out with Tom. "I've absolutely got to work on my poem," she told him. "I've hardly even looked at it and I'm supposed to recite in front of my whole English class."

"Read me a little of it," Tom suggested. "Then I'll study film classics and leave you alone."

Elizabeth leafed to the right page.

"If thou must love me, let it be for nought
Except for love's sake only. Do not say

'I love her for her smile—her look—her way
Of speaking gently,—for a trick of thought . . .' "

She didn't get any further, because Tom was leaning over her shoulder, tickling her cheek with his.

"Don't," she said unconvincingly. "That's not the end of the stanza."

"But I have to prove to you I love you for love's sake only," he said, turning her face to his and softly brushing her lips with his.

Elizabeth sighed, half closing her eyes. She let herself kiss him for another second before she pushed him away. "Let's face it—our studying is not going well. It's not even going. We can't do this together."

Tom pulled back and looked at her for a moment. "I'll leave you alone if you want. You know that."

"But I don't want you to." Elizabeth smiled. "That's the problem." She got up and collected Tom's books, then put them in his hands. "I'll see you tomorrow."

"You're very cruel," Tom said with a sigh. "What if tomorrow never comes?"

Elizabeth looked into his eyes. She wasn't sure if he was joking. Tom had been through so much in his life, she knew tomorrow was something he never took for granted. One morning two years ago he had woken up as a young man with an older sister, a little brother, and two parents. By that night they were all dead, killed in a car crash. He was alone. That was why it had been so hard for him to love her. He hadn't ever wanted to love anyone again—he had been afraid he would lose them.

"I promise tomorrow will come," she said softly. "Nothing will ever happen to me."

"OK," he whispered, resting his chin on top of her head. "You do seem to lead a charmed life." Then he moved his mouth to hers. Just as Elizabeth was closing her eyes and sinking into the depths of a good-bye kiss, an envelope slid under the door.

"What's that?" Tom asked.

Elizabeth reluctantly let go of him and reached down for the envelope. The plain sheet of notebook paper inside said only, *You are mine*.

"Todd's early for Valentine's Day," Tom remarked, obviously annoyed.

"Why would Todd do this?" Elizabeth frowned. "He *knows* I'm not his."

"I'm not so sure." Tom shrugged.

Elizabeth read the note again. The bold, slightly messy letters didn't look familiar. She would recognize Todd's handwriting. Who else would write her a love note?

"I wonder . . ." Elizabeth shook her head. "Todd lives in the new residence hall near the library since he got kicked out of the jock dorm."

"Yeah, so?" Tom scowled.

"Well, that's all the way across campus. I wonder where he was calling from a minute ago."

Celine blew a smoke ring. It hovered tranquilly over her bath. She sank deeper into the hot, soothing water, sticking her red-lacquered toenails just out of the bubbles.

"My aching feet," she murmured. "My poor, unloved, overworked aching feet." Celine closed her eyes and let her free hand float to the top of the water, luxuriating in the silence.

"Waah-screek!"

Like liquid metal, the sound seared between her ears. The smoke ring disintegrated in fright. Celine dropped her cigarette in the water.

"Aaaaaah!" she wailed, and not only because a wet cigarette was an unpleasant thing to have in the tub. She had thought she'd left hell behind in the cafeteria. All afternoon, she'd stirred slop, mopped up spilled slop, and poured slop in bowls to be eaten by the unwary. Instead she had only exchanged the kitchen for a new hell. Saxophone hell. Celine stood in the soapy water and listened again.

"He *is* playing in his bathroom!" she shrieked.

Celine hastily dried off, wrapped her robe with the plunging neckline as high around her as it would go, and marched out of her apartment.

She banged furiously on her neighbor's door. The sound changed from squeaking to scales. Up and down, up and down, holding on some notes, fancifully skipping ahead on others. She pounded again.

Abruptly the noise stopped. A moment later the door was flung open. Celine stifled a gasp. She was immediately sorry she hadn't tried her new burgundy lipstick before coming over.

Her saxophone-playing neighbor had rumpled dark-brown hair, gray eyes, and the biggest shoulders west of the Mississippi, and probably east of it too. He still carried his shiny brass instrument, attached by a strap to his neck, and he wore a maroon sweatshirt that said SWARTHMORE across the front. Why had she assumed he would be short and nerdy, like her other neighbor, the biologist?

"Can you tell me"—she stopped to clear her throat—"why you're blowing that thing in the bathroom?"

"The acoustics are best in there," he said calmly.

Celine propped herself against the door frame. "Oh, really."

"I'm Matt Torres," the guy said, raising an eyebrow. "I've seen you going in and out of the building with shopping bags."

This was a positive sign. Being noticed was always the first step on the way to an invitation. "My name is Celine Boudreaux," she said, pouting her full lips and dripping honey into her accent. "I'm from Louisiana."

Celine smiled and leaned closer to him, which caused her robe to accidentally fall open a little. He would also be able to smell her bubble bath. Bubble bath wasn't as good as Chanel, of course, but it might give him the idea: sweet-smelling girl, pretty girl, right next door and available . . .

Matt had his arms crossed over his chest. "My girlfriend goes to Swarthmore, in Pennsylvania," he said pointedly. "She's studying oboe."

Celine bit back the urge to say something uncomplimentary about oboe players. Suddenly she was hungry for friends, any friends, and this guy could be a start. "My boyfriend's away too," she told him.

"Where does he go to school?" Matt asked, sounding somewhat interested.

"Um—he's in the foreign service." *Very foreign*, she thought. *Very far away.*

"I'll be playing for another hour," Matt said curtly. "I have a concert coming up I have to practice for."

"I just love music," Celine said sweetly. "You go right ahead and play. I do believe I'll be at your concert, too."

"Good night." Matt looked a little more friendly as he closed the door.

"'Night now." Celine padded back to her apartment, definitely cheered. As the saxophone went back to tooting scales, she saw prospects on the horizon. A girlfriend that far away might as well be dead. "Maybe he would serenade the ever-irritating Elizabeth if I asked him to," she said to herself, opening her door. "Maybe at four in the morning, if I could get him up with the biologist."

Her bubble bath would be stone cold by now, so Celine lay on the couch in the tiny living room that doubled as her bedroom. She lit another cigarette and thought about Matt. He had a cool, arrogant look that reminded her favorably of William's. Dear William.

Suddenly inspired, Celine got up and rummaged in her desk for a piece of scented stationery. She didn't know where William was, but she had his parents' address. Time to renew an old acquaintance. Celine had no doubt that William would soon be free again, and she wanted to be the first person at SVU to greet him.

Chapter Five

"No, thank you," Lila said to the stewardess, her English sounding strange in her ears. "I don't drink." It would take more booze than was available on the planet to drown her sorrow.

She and her mother sat in the first-class section of a 747, flying direct from Rome to Los Angeles. Black sunglasses hid Lila's puffy eyes. If only her black clothes hid her completely.

At first she had thrown temper tantrums after the accident. *"Non mi serve niente! Non mi serve nessuno!"* "I don't need anything! I don't need anybody!" she had screamed at the servants, then her aunt, and finally her parents, who had flown over the day after the accident. Mr. Fowler was planning to spend the next few days with Tisiano's lawyers, dealing with the complexities of death and estates. Lila wanted only to get as far from Italy as possible. She couldn't stand to be in the home she had shared with Tisiano. Her mother had booked her on the first flight out.

What was she supposed to do now, after her life as an Italian countess? Lila nervously opened a packet of airline peanuts and poured them out on her tray. Mrs. Fowler, sitting next to her, was chatting away about college. She had already enrolled Lila to audit courses for the rest of the semester at Sweet Valley University, majoring in psychology, of all things. Lila supposed going to college was all right. Anything was all right.

She didn't care. She had to park herself somewhere just to pass the time, but she couldn't imagine that life would ever be fun or inspiring again.

"Vorrei che fosse qui," she said quietly, scattering the peanuts across the tray and ignoring her mother's sympathetic look. *I wish you were here. My darling, darling Tisiano. Oh, God.* In just a few hours she would be back in Sweet Valley. It felt as if she had never lived there, as if the people there were no more than characters in a movie she had once seen. Strange, English-speaking people who moved jerkily about under a blue cardboard sky.

Except for Jessica. Lila settled deeper in the posh leather of the seat and closed her eyes. She would talk, really talk to Jessica for the first time in months. She and Jessica had always understood each other. That was one comforting thought.

"Vadi a casa," Lila said wearily, the tears still sliding down her cheeks as she began to doze off. *I am going home.*

The psychiatrist wore an immaculate white coat. His office smelled of formaldehyde and ink. "You're not cooperating, William," he said. "You'll learn that cooperation is very important at the Harrington Institution."

William sprawled in a chair and silently smoked. He fixed the doctor with an insolent stare.

"How do you feel about your parents for committing you?"

William examined the lit tip of his cigarette.

"All right," the psychiatrist said, watching him but pretending not to. "You'll change your mind about talking after you've been here for a while. Let me explain how the grounds are laid out so that you'll feel more at home." He pushed a map across the desk toward William. "Here is the temporary-care facility. Most of the patients who are housed there have relatively manageable problems and will be released in less than two months. The extended-care facility is for patients with more intractable problems—"

"Raving lunatics," William said suddenly.

The doctor ignored this. "A beautiful gorge

surrounds the institution, and we have picnic benches overlooking the view for those patients who have earned our trust. As for activities—"

"How deep is the gorge?" William asked abruptly.

"Three hundred feet. It is a security measure to protect our patients. They should not at this time intermingle with the general community." The doctor leaned back in his chair and looked at William intently.

"So you'd like me to believe this is a country club," William sneered. "I still call it a jail."

"You're here for a reason, William. Until you are rehabilitated, you belong under the care of trained personnel. Some of the patients respond better to treatment than others. Those patients are released sooner."

"How did I do on those ink-blot tests?" William asked suddenly.

The doctor smiled an eerie, mirthless smile. "You did fine," he said.

William laughed. He had looked through the contents of the doctor's desk before the doctor had entered the office, and he had found the folder with his test results. It had been stamped DISTURBED AND DANGEROUS.

"Now, let's talk about how you'll spend your time," the psychiatrist went on. "You won't be bored if you take part in the many activities we plan daily for our patients."

"Basket weaving," William said. He could feel a cold fury building somewhere near his lungs. He had to slow his breathing to compensate.

"You're being sarcastic, William, which we don't appreciate," the doctor snapped. "The arts and crafts the patients do are *therapy*."

"Therapy," William said mockingly. "I understand. I can hardly wait."

"You won't be eligible for most of the activities for a while anyway," the psychiatrist said. "Because of the nature of your crimes, you'll be remanded for an indeterminate time to the D ward."

"And what does that mean?" William flicked his lighter. A small blue-and-orange flame was born. The flame burned stronger. It would be so easy to set all these books and papers on fire, and the psychiatrist with them. William enjoyed the idea.

"You'll be confined to the locked ward unless you are under supervision. It's where we put the dangerous patients," the psychiatrist said. "You'll be there for a long time, I think."

Alex opened her door warily. A dark shape clutching a bottle lurched forward, falling against the door frame.

"Todd?" Alex asked disbelievingly. "Where have you been?"

Without being invited, Todd stumbled past

her. Once he was under the light in her room, Alex could see that his hair was standing on end, his face was scratched and smudged with something gray, and he had a big rip across the back of his jacket. She relieved him of his bottle. Scotch whiskey, eighty-seven proof.

This was really weird. As long as Alex had known Todd, he had always been the perfect, clean-cut, all-American jock. Now he was sloshed on a Tuesday night. She set the bottle on her desk and turned back to him.

"She said she'd call, Alex!" Todd slurred, throwing himself into a chair. "She didn't, dammit, and I waited for hours."

Of course. Alex should have known it was about Elizabeth. She drew a sharp, careful breath. She was trying very hard not to cry over her own problems. After all, now that she was single again, she didn't want to destroy her appearance with red eyes and blotched skin.

But her looks were shot anyway, Alex thought, glancing in the mirror. She no longer saw a healthy, glowing college woman. There were shadows under her eyes, and she hadn't washed her hair in almost a week. The mirror showed a haunted woman. An abandoned woman.

"I don't know what I'll do if she keeps this up," Todd said. He sounded totally out of control.

Alex pulled the extra chair next to him and

laid her hand over his. "I know it's really hard," she said.

"I deserve this." Todd slumped forward, rubbing his eyes. "I treated her like a doormat when we first came to SVU."

Yeah, you did, Alex agreed silently.

"I remember that day she stopped by and saw Lauren in my room," Todd went on. "She was so upset."

It wasn't exactly that Lauren was in your room, Alex thought. *It was the fact that she was holding a toothbrush and wearing nothing but your practice jersey.* Alex had heard all about it from Mark. Mark said Todd had just let Elizabeth rush off in tears, to commit suicide or beg in the streets or something. Alex felt a pang. And what had she done to help Elizabeth?

Todd retrieved the scotch and began drinking it right out of the bottle, jerking it up for a quick hit every time he thought of something he'd messed up, Alex figured. Pathetic.

She wasn't doing much better. For the thousandth time, Alex remembered her own last "date" with Mark, the day before he dumped her for basketball and L.A.

She'd asked him to go for a drive, hoping they could park somewhere nice and talk. When they had first started going out, they'd spent hours parked at the ocean, at scenic overlooks, and in the school lot. Sometimes they'd kissed and talked until dawn, about sports and college and love or whatever.

On their last date they had met at a restaurant, but Mark hadn't really wanted to talk, not to her. At first he'd stared sullenly at the wall. That had been loads of fun. Then he'd started talking about his tryout in L.A., the NBA, and the girls he was going to get.

Alex had tried to change the subject to something more interesting and less threatening to herself, but he'd turned on her.

"What the hell do you want from me?" he shouted, so loud that everyone in the restaurant had turned around. "You can leave if you don't like the conversation!"

Alex rubbed her cheeks, which felt stiff from too much crying. Maybe the next time she would have the strength to leave, and not go crawling back to him. If she ever saw him again.

She got up and walked closer to the mirror. Slowly, closing her eyes, she kissed her reflection. A perfect round, red lipstick smudge remained when she leaned back.

What happened to my perfect life? Alex wondered, pressing her forehead against the mirror. *When did it all go down the toilet?*

Todd held his head in his hands. "Now what, Alex?" he asked flatly. "I can't get on with my life—I've tried for days. I feel like I need to *do* something to get Elizabeth back."

Alex looked at him sympathetically. Then her face hardened. *Elizabeth makes everyone fall apart,* she thought. *Elizabeth and her TV reporter games.* By reporting on the sports scandal, Elizabeth had destroyed the lives of at least half the basketball team, including Mark's. And hers.

Alex and Elizabeth had been best friends for years, until a couple of months ago. Alex knew that Elizabeth didn't care at all if people were hurt by what she reported. Elizabeth was interested only in truth.

Alex took the bottle and poured a small shot of Todd's scotch. She hadn't had even a glass of wine in a week, but right now a drink seemed like the answer to her problems. At least it would help her to relax.

She poured a slug of scotch into a water glass and handed it to Todd.

"I'm glad you're drinking with me," Todd said, raising his tormented eyes to hers. "I don't want to drink alone."

Alex grabbed her glass and held it up. She glanced at the scotch and saw that half the bottle was left. "Cheers," she said. "Here's to college life."

On Wednesday Nina walked quickly along the path to her physics class. Normally, she would be as happy as it was possible for her to be. She had aced a big exam yesterday, and the professor had called to congratulate her. "I think we may have a budding Einstein in this class," he had said admiringly.

But Nina wasn't at all happy. And she had just seen the reason, turning a corner of Oakley Hall and headed right for her. Nina had skipped the BSU meeting on Monday night to study for the physics test. She had told herself that Bryan wouldn't really be mad at her. It was just one little meeting. And the physics exam was so important to her.

But as Tuesday wore on, she'd realized he was avoiding her. She didn't see him anywhere all day. Usually she saw him several times: at the snack bar, or waiting for her after her psych class, or crossing the quad on the way to friends, classes, or meetings. He didn't call that evening, either.

Bryan marched toward her along the path. Well, it looked as though the stalemate was about to end right now. Maybe they could at least be civil.

Bryan caught up to her in the center of the quad. Nina waited, feeling doomed. "Hi," she said.

Bryan said nothing, walking by her.

"Hi," Nina said again.

Bryan stopped and faced her. "You are one messed-up girl."

Nina's mouth dropped open.

"You still don't get where your priorities should be—*have* to be."

"I *have* to get into graduate school," Nina said quietly, although her voice trembled. His expression frightened her. She could hardly recognize this cold face. It seemed incredible that they had ever even kissed.

"Look at your friends!" he shouted. "I'm the only *black* acquaintance you even have."

"Now we're just acquaintances?" Nina said, hurt.

"I feel like I don't know you at all," he replied.

Nina was scared she was going to burst into tears. "Why are you doing this?" she demanded. "My mother's been yelling at me for weeks because I'm wasting time on BSU activities when I should be studying. Now you're on my case because you think I study too much. I guess both of you agree that I shouldn't have any friends." Of course, Bryan wasn't saying exactly that. He was saying that she shouldn't have any *white* friends. Her mother didn't want her to have radical friends of any color. So who was she allowed to be friends with?

"Why shouldn't I hang around with Elizabeth?" Nina asked angrily, tears welling in her eyes. "She's the only person in my life who doesn't criticize every move I make." Nina tried to wipe away the tears. She never remembered to carry tissues. But then, until she had met

87

Bryan, she had hardly ever *needed* them.

"You don't care about me as a person," she said unsteadily. "You just see me as a number or something. A body that has to be at your meetings."

"Nina, you're really good at theoretical subjects," Bryan said, starting to walk off. "But you don't deal too well with reality."

The phone rang. Jessica sat up quickly, wiping her eyes. She wondered how long she had been sprawled on her bed in the darkened room, crying. *I should have gone to see Mike,* she thought. *It probably would have been awful, but it still would have been better than lying here, eaten alive by guilt.* Jessica had taken a two-hour drive on Monday instead, circling the university and then several shopping malls. She had just felt lonelier than ever.

She picked up the phone with a sniffle. "Hello?"

"Jessica?"

"Lila!" Jessica had never been so happy to hear from her friend. "How are you? How's Italy?"

"I'm not in Italy—I'm in Sweet Valley."

"But . . . why? Is something wrong?"

"Oh, Jess, everything is wrong." Lila gave a small sob.

She sounds just like me, Jessica thought. *Did her count run away?* "What happened?" she asked cautiously. She didn't want to be as prying and tactless as people had been about her problems.

"Tisiano is dead," Lila said in a wobbly voice. "He was in a boating accident. I'm a widow. So I've come back here—there's nothing for me in Italy anymore."

"Oh, Lila." A fresh stream of tears coursed down Jessica's cheeks. "I'm so, so sorry."

Lila gave a long sigh. "Thanks, Jess. I'm totally cried out about it, at least for now. But what have you been doing? How's your husband, and the Thetas, and Liz?"

Jessica burst into sobs.

"What, Jessica?" Lila asked gently. "When I didn't hear from you for so long, I just assumed you were too busy with married life to write. Did something go wrong?"

"I almost wrote you about it." Jessica dried her tears on the edge of the pillow. "But I didn't want to send you a letter that was so completely sad."

"Jess, what happened?" Lila asked.

Jessica took a deep breath. "Mike didn't treat me very well, especially after we were married, and Steven got upset about it. They had a couple of fights. Then Mike came after me with a gun, and he and Steven fought again, and—" Jessica choked.

"And what?" Lila asked. "You can tell me."

"Mike got shot," Jessica said in a rush. "He'll never walk again."

"God," Lila gasped. "That's hard, Jess. So are you . . . taking care of him?"

"Not exactly. Mike and I are both trying to get the marriage annulled."

"Oh," Lila said. Jessica wondered if Lila thought she was completely cruel for leaving Mike when he was helpless.

"So, well, needless to say, my life hasn't been going that smoothly," Jessica hurried on. "Liz is doing great, though. I've moved back in with her."

Lila sighed. "God. Can you believe what we've been through since we saw each other last summer?" Lila sounded a little more like her old self.

"When can you come over?" Jessica asked.

"I'm resting up from jet lag today, but I could visit tomorrow afternoon," Lila said. "I've got to register to audit the rest of the semester. Then next spring, I'll be a real student, I guess. I don't know, Jessica. I just don't know what I want to do right now. But I can't sit around and think all the time. Anything would be better than that."

"I know how you feel," Jessica said. They were both silent for a minute.

"So I'll see you tomorrow," Lila said, sounding a little happier.

"Just come up to my room, 28 Dickenson," Jessica said. "I'll give you the complete tour: dorms, Theta house, campus hangouts." She felt better. It would be kind of fun to play the big sister with Lila, showing her the university and where to go.

"Sounds like a plan," Lila said. *"Ciao."*

After they had hung up, Jessica sat thinking for a few minutes. Then she brushed her hair and inspected the small amount of makeup she wore. She looked a lot prettier than she felt.

I'll go see Mike right now, she thought, grabbing her car keys. *Then it won't be on my mind tomorrow when I'm trying to have fun for the first time in weeks. This time, I absolutely will go.*

Chapter Six

Winston moved carefully toward Denise at the door of the humanities building. He kissed her cheek. That went well. Her look was soft and affectionate. He sighed with relief.

He still had to plan these things. Sometimes he had the feeling that it was his spontaneity that had gotten him into trouble in the past.

Encouraged, Winston put his lips to hers. He closed his eyes, and white sunlight sparkled behind his eyelids. Then there was a loud snort.

Winston opened his eyes and found himself looking directly into the sun behind Denise's head. It formed a blinding halo around the face of Bruce Patman.

"I didn't know you and Egbert were dating," Bruce sneered.

"You never asked," Denise replied.

Bruce shrugged. Obviously who Winston

dated didn't matter at all, since Winston himself didn't matter.

He watched Bruce warily, afraid that another embarrassing high school story was coming up. But Bruce turned to Denise. "So, we've got a date Saturday?" he asked, smiling that big-man-on-campus, I'm-in-control-here smile that Winston hated so much.

"Sure," Denise said. "Over at the Sigma house, about eight."

Bruce smiled. "I'll be there. Don't bother to eat—I'll fix us something." He sauntered off.

Winston sighed. He definitely would have preferred stories from the past to this. He would have preferred death.

Denise was sensitive enough to notice his distress. "Bruce and I have to work on our class project, Win," she said. "Chill."

"You already worked on it," Winston said. Fear was giving him major heartburn. "Yesterday after class. That's why you were late to dinner."

"We didn't *finish* the project, Winnie," Denise said patiently. "We're going to be working on it for at least the next week, probably. Look, I've got to go to class. Bye!" She kissed him quickly and disappeared into the building.

Winston stared after her. *She's the most beautiful girl on campus,* he thought. *Maybe in the world. What chance have I got against a guy like*

Bruce? Winston could already hear the sound of his heart breaking.

Steven picked up a small bowl made out of a gourd and felt a wave of sadness wash over him. It was Billie's—she had forgotten it.

He still couldn't believe she'd moved out. Just couldn't believe it. He knew he'd made her mad many times in the past, but never like this.

The apartment looked empty, even though most of the furniture was still there. But most of the paintings were gone from the walls. So was the old, colorful Oriental rug they'd had on the living room floor.

Steven set the gourd on the kitchen counter and dialed Clarissa's number, the friend Billie was staying with for the time being. "Hi," he said when Billie answered.

"Hello, Steven," she said. "What now?"

"What do you mean?"

"You called just an hour ago."

"Well—" Steven gripped the phone hard. "I just wanted to ask you . . . to ask you to come back. Please?"

"Not now."

"Please," he said again, trying not to sound angry.

"No, Steven." Her voice was rising. "We've been over all this."

"But I don't understand why you left."

"Maybe you should try listening," she said. "Excuse me. Rob?" she yelled to somebody. "Get the door, please!"

"Who was that?" Steven demanded.

"Rob," Billie said. "He lives here."

"I thought you were just living with Clarissa." Steven swallowed hard.

"With Clarissa and Rob and Allan. They pay the rent, too. Don't be upset."

"Why should I be upset just because you're living with a bunch of guys?" Steven shouted.

"Look, Steven," Billie said coldly. "I've got to go."

"Yeah, I've got to go too." Steven banged down the phone. "This is Mike's fault," he muttered as he headed for the door. "I don't want to rehabilitate him; I want to kill him."

He stomped down the stairs to Mike's floor. "I almost did kill him," he said. "He wants me to kill him now. Where does this all leave me?"

Girlfriendless, for one thing. Billie didn't want to move back in until he had gotten over what she called his "lunatic" relationship with Mike and had more time for her. But he wouldn't have any extra time until Mike could take care of himself, which Mike didn't want to do at all.

Steven let himself into Mike's apartment. In the living room he could hear furious gunfire from a Western on TV. Mike was sprawled on the couch. The room was dark, except for the wavering light from the black-and-white movie.

"Are you watching that thing or just being a vegetable?" Steven asked.

"I didn't feel like going skiing today, so I settled for the next-best thing," Mike said sourly.

Steven flicked on the overhead lights. Mike swore, predictably. Steven shrugged. "You haven't done jack for weeks," he said. "If you'd do your exercises, you'd feel better."

"You really are all hearts and flowers," Mike sneered.

Maybe if he hated me enough, he'd get off his butt, Steven thought. "You can't have your pain medication unless you do some exercises," he bargained. A little voice in his head told him he was a real creep, but he ignored it.

"I like pain." Mike rumpled his hair and continued to stare at the screen.

Steven reached over the back of the couch and grabbed the remote. He switched off the TV.

The next second he couldn't breathe. Mike's hands, clumsy but still strong, were around his neck, choking him. Steven threw himself backward and managed to break the hold. Mike fell back on the couch, then rolled off onto the floor.

Steven stared at him in horror. It was bad enough that he was expected to touch Mike's arms and legs, and help him from furniture into the wheelchair. Now he had to pick him up and carry him? Mike would probably spit and bite.

I can't just leave him there, though, Steven thought. Mike was struggling to sit up. Again Steven felt pity he didn't want to feel. Then he remembered that if the night nurse thought he had neglected Mike, he could go to jail.

"OK, buddy," he said. "Let me help you up." Mike stiffened.

"You hate me as much as I hate you, don't you?" Steven asked, bending over him. "What did I ever do to you? Just tried to keep my little sister out of your sleazy hands. Is that a crime?"

"You turned her against me," Mike said through gritted teeth. "You broke up my marriage and you don't give a damn."

"Well, you've done wonders for my home life too." Steven stepped forward and seized Mike under the arms. "Now get back on the couch."

Mike went limp. The deadweight was more than Steven could handle, and he dropped Mike back on the floor.

He's never going to be able to take care of himself, Steven thought, beginning to despair. He had never felt this way before. He couldn't control what was happening. Billie had slipped away from him, and somehow Mike was too.

Summoning all his strength, Steven heaved Mike back onto the couch. *What's going to slip away from me next?* he wondered.

*　　*　　*

Jessica knocked softly at Mike's door. She could hear the whang of gunfire and thundering hooves on the TV.

"Bring me a drink!" Mike ordered.

"Anything you say, O Most High," Jessica heard a sarcastic voice answer.

Jessica gasped. Steven was there! Alarms shrieked in her head. She turned immediately to leave. *The last time the three of us were together, somebody almost died,* she thought. She had no desire to relive that night. *I don't think they heard me knock. I'll come back another time,* she told herself.

She walked quickly down the hall, but her footsteps slowed. Finally, reluctantly, she stopped altogether on the top step of the stairway to freedom.

Tomorrow she was seeing Lila, who was still carrying around a lot of grief but was ready to start over. Jessica wanted to resolve things with Mike so that her own life would be like that. If she didn't see him now, her guilt would start tearing her apart again.

Just remember, this time nobody has a gun, Jessica reminded herself as she knocked at Mike's door. Mike's gun was safely in a police vault downtown.

Steven whipped open the door. "Jessica!" he said, obviously amazed. "What are you—" Then he shook his head, lifted his hands, and stepped away from the door.

Jessica walked into the apartment, trying not to panic. She knew the place so well, it seemed strange that she didn't belong here anymore. There was the living room, with its afghan carpets and the oversized sofa and armchairs, the bookshelves, the stereo. The big green ceiling fan was still. It was so dark, she longed to throw on all the lights. But this wasn't her apartment anymore. Besides, what would she see with more light?

Steven passed her, carrying a glass of water. In a moment he was back. "I'm out of here," he said. "Would you stay another fifteen minutes until the night nurse comes on? Thanks, Jess, you're a lifesaver."

Not exactly, Jessica thought. *Just look at what happened to Mike.* "Why are you in such a hurry?" she asked nervously.

Steven laughed and shrugged. "Nothing much. Billie's moved out, so it's not like I'm rushing into someone's arms. It's just I've had enough of our invalid there." He jerked a thumb toward the living room. "You'll see."

"Oh, OK," Jessica stammered, trying to hide her shock. Steven and Billie had broken up? They had been practically engaged. But this didn't seem the time or the place to get into it.

Steven let himself out, and Jessica walked

slowly into the darkness of the living room. "Mike?" she whispered.

No answer. Mike lay almost sideways on the couch, watching TV. John Wayne galloped on a horse toward hundreds of warring Apaches, about to save the day.

He can move a little, can't he? Jessica thought, horrified. Mike's body was thin and unrecognizable under a blanket. She made herself get a grip. "How are you feeling?" she asked in a level voice. Cheerfulness was beyond her.

John Wayne ordered the troops to assume fighting position, but other than that, the room was silent.

"I would have come before." Her voice broke. She leaned over the back of the couch. "But I'm really behind on classes . . . and . . ."

Mike continued to stare at the TV. Jessica gave a trembly sigh. This wasn't working—he'd heard all her excuses before. She turned to leave.

"I don't know why you came at all." His voice followed her into the foyer. Jessica stopped, her hand on her mouth.

"Oh, by the way, I can still hear," he said. "I heard you and your brother's discussion of my personality. He can . . ." Mike hesitated. "He can leave me alone. And so can you. I set you free, remember?"

"Yes," Jessica said softly. "I remember."

"So get out." Mike's voice was harsh.

Jessica opened the front door and eased herself out. Silent sobs forced their way through her throat. *Is there really such a thing as a good cry?* she wondered. Down the hall she saw the night nurse arriving, her starched white uniform glaring like a lightbulb.

From the other side of the door Jessica heard Mike's own quiet sobbing.

"Celine?" asked a shy, hoarse voice.

Celine put her key in the lock and turned with a dazzling, tipsy smile. She had been trying to meet the biologist next door for days, and finally, here he was.

She had listened for him at four A.M. That was his usual time to go to sleep or get up—she wasn't sure which—but suddenly he'd changed his schedule. She had thought she heard him coming in at midnight once or twice, but before she could pounce, he'd switched the timing of his trips again.

So she had found out his name from the chairman of the biology department. Then she taped a note to his lab station, asking him to meet her here tonight.

Celine had spent the first part of the night sharing a bottle of wine with Peter Wilbourne at Sigma house. They'd talked about happier days, when Peter had been president of the fraternity and neither of them had studied at all. But the evening had been a total bore. Now that Peter wasn't president of anything, he was about as exciting as day-old toast. Celine had been glad to hurry back for her appointment with her nerdy neighbor.

"Well, I have been looking for *you*!" she drawled, clutching the doorknob for balance. "You're a hard man to catch."

"I put my flies on a new schedule," he explained. He stuck out a hand and shook hers vigorously. "Paul Richards. I already know who you are."

Celine couldn't believe she was going to stick around for more of this, but she did. She needed him because he was a science major. He was going to help her make a stink bomb to put in Elizabeth's room, although he didn't know it yet.

"And just how did you find out who I am?" she purred. She had already gotten an earful about him from the chairman of the biology department. Paul was a double biology-mathematics major, with a grade-point average of 4.0.

Celine just hadn't known how to express her admiration.

"You told me who you are in your note," he reminded her, moving a little closer. "And I've seen you around campus."

Celine hadn't seen him or, really, any biology

major up close before. Paul had taken off his glasses. He had golden brown eyes like a fox, blond-streaked brown hair, and a full beard and mustache. Because he was only a little taller than she was, she could look right into his animal eyes.

He wasn't that bad, actually. Especially if you were desperate.

Celine smiled again. "You have flies?"

"Fruit flies." Paul shifted uneasily, as if mentioning his pets made him miss them.

Celine opened her door. "Come on in for a quick cup of coffee. I must hear about these flies."

Paul didn't need any more encouragement. "I'm experimenting to see how different mutations are inherited," he said, practically walking on her heels. "Some of the mutations I'm following are white eyes, curly wings, and dumpy body."

William has white eyes, Nina has curly wings, and Elizabeth has a dumpy body, Celine thought, trying to focus on the cappuccino maker. She giggled.

"What's funny?" Paul asked.

"I know a lot of people with those mutations," Celine said, resisting the urge to slide onto the floor and laugh at her joke until she cried. *Elizabeth Dumpy Body Wakefield.*

Paul laughed obligingly. "Yeah, maybe I

know them too. The mutations might have a similar genetic basis in humans and flies . . ."

He trailed her into the kitchen, talking steady fruit flies. Celine thanked God the roar of the cappuccino maker finally drowned him out.

She handed him his mug and led him to the couch, kicking her orange pumps into the corner as she went.

Paul gulped his cappuccino as if it were the fifty-cent bilge Celine helped make all day at the cafeteria instead of French roast Café du Monde from New Orleans. In between gulps he talked nonstop about somebody named Mendel, genes, and a loathsome little worm everybody studied called Nematoda. The steamed milk got in his mustache and beard.

Celine hoped he thought her half-closed eyes meant she was fascinated with what he was saying, rather than bored out of her skull. *Amazing*, she thought. *He outtalks my granny, the world's champion talker, by at least five words to one. I wonder how long it's been since he spoke to another human being.*

"I follow the mutations through several generations," Paul went on, slurping up the last of his cappuccino.

"So you get more and more flies all the time," Celine said, suddenly waking from her stupor. "Do they eat a lot?"

"Almost nothing," Paul assured her. "Just a

little of this blue sugar mixture we put in the bottom of the test tubes."

Flies everywhere, Celine thought, shifting upright on the couch. *Flies in Elizabeth's moisturizer, flies in her eyes. Flies eating her granola. They might live forever on that.*

Celine suddenly grabbed Paul's shirt collar and pulled him close to her. Then she kissed him, long and luxuriously.

Just to make sure he comes back, she thought.

Chapter Seven

"Neither love me for
Thine own dear pity's wiping my cheeks dry,—
A creature might forget to weep, who bore
Thy comfort long, and lose thy love thereby!"

Elizabeth recited the poem, quickly French-braiding her hair. In about eight minutes she had to recite it from memory in front of her whole English class. She'd be lucky if she could even get it out, much less with the right expression.

She tied a black bow at the end of her braid and hurried to the door. She was out of breath by the time she'd made it across the quad. But at least being constantly late and forgetful was making her burn up a lot of calories—she might never have to worry about her weight again. She arrived at the humanities building two minutes before her class was scheduled to start.

"Liz?"

Elizabeth whirled and saw Todd sitting to the side of the door. He looked angry.

Elizabeth's hand flew to her throat. She had forgotten all about Todd. But obviously he hadn't forgotten her.

"Hi," she said, trying to reach around him for the door. His face was red and splotchy; he must have been waiting in the sun a long time.

"Liz—" Todd stood up. "Where have you been? I must have left you six messages over the past two days."

Elizabeth sighed. "I know, and I'm sorry. But, Todd, my class is starting now. You have to—" Move? She couldn't think how to tell him that he just had to move. "You have to wait," she finished. "I'll call you when I have a spare second."

"I've heard that line before," Todd said angrily. "You won't."

Elizabeth opened her mouth for an angry retort, but stopped herself. She didn't have time for an argument. Besides . . . was Todd drunk? She thought she smelled alcohol on his breath. That might explain why his face was so red.

She had to get away from him. What was left for her to say? She didn't know when she would get to the story on the university. It was starting to look like she never would—she could barely keep up with her classwork.

"We really need to talk," Todd said sadly.

Elizabeth was getting desperate. He was standing right in her way. While he was dumping on her, she was about to fail English. "Saturday," she said quickly. "Saturday night we'll have coffee and straighten everything out."

Todd looked skeptical. "Do you promise?"

"Of course."

Todd nodded and moved away from the door. She noticed his movements were a little shaky, and she felt a pang of guilt. Todd was usually so sure of himself. He had always moved with an athlete's grace.

One thing at a time, she told herself as she ran flat out for her English class. Frantically mumbling her poem, she entered the room one step behind the professor.

"Ah, Ms. Wakefield," Professor Martin said. "I believe we have you down as first to recite."

Elizabeth nodded and walked to the center of the classroom. For a second, looking out at all the expectant faces of her classmates frightened her. Then in her mind she saw Tom's face, the night he had confessed his love for her. She closed her eyes and began, her heart reciting the words.

"But love me for love's sake, that evermore
Thou mayst love on, through love's eternity . . ."

She finished and looked up. She had completely forgotten the class was there.

"Lovely, Ms. Wakefield," the professor applauded. Elizabeth smiled and took her seat. *Thanks, Tom,* she thought. She turned to the first page of her notebook and wrote, "I love Tom." *My fairy-tale prince,* she thought. *I always dreamed I'd meet someone like him.* When Elizabeth was little, she had drawn hearts and filled them in with the names of cool guys she didn't know. She had been waiting to put Tom in those hearts all her life. She wrote: "My love for you is my happiness." Dumb, but true. So what if love was turning her into a moron?

Tom had once written her a wonderful poem, although he had left it unsigned at first. That had been a mistake, because William White had claimed to have written it and she'd believed him for months. She really should have known, though, that such passion and love could have come from only Tom.

Elizabeth wondered if she could write him a poem back. In high school she had been a decent poet. She closed her eyes, trying to find the right words. . . .

The guy behind her was shoving her elbow. Elizabeth opened her eyes with a jolt.

"Ms. Wakefield?" the professor asked. "I said, What do you think is the treachery Byron had in mind when he wrote his poem 'When We Two Parted'?"

"Um . . . infidelity?" Elizabeth guessed.

"Perhaps," the professor said, nodding thoughtfully. "See me after class, please."

Now I've blown it, Elizabeth thought. Still, she couldn't stop herself from doodling a pair of kissing hearts, one red, one blue. Then she flipped to a fresh page.

We'll be together soon, was written in black block letters.

Elizabeth smiled. Tom had wanted to surprise her with a little love note.

But how could it be from Tom? she wondered. *When did he manage to sneak my notebook away to write that?*

The strange thing was, the handwriting looked the same as that in the note shoved under her door two days ago. Had Tom gotten someone to deliver the first note as some kind of game? She doubted it; he hadn't liked that first note at all.

Elizabeth sighed with exasperation. Todd? He couldn't get to her notebooks. Tom *must* be writing the notes. Of course he was. Somehow. She went back to writing her poem.

Professor Martin cleared his throat loudly. Elizabeth looked around. Apparently class had been over for a while. All the other students had left.

"That was a touching rendition of Browning's

111

sonnet," he said. "Can I convince you to recite another poem at the Literary Club's meeting this Saturday night?"

"Sure," Elizabeth said absently, getting up and stacking her books. *I guess I can do that*, she thought. *At least I didn't get busted for being a space cadet.*

"I've got my one-week anniversary with Elizabeth all planned," Tom said to Danny, propping his feet up on his dorm room bed.

"Something tells me I'm going to hear all about it," Danny said mockingly. He dropped the book he was reading. "Are you flying to Paris?"

"No." Tom wondered for a second if that was something he should have considered. He suddenly felt uncertain about all his plans. "Which do you think—Mexican or seafood?" he asked.

"Mexican," Danny said. "But I could go either way."

"I'm not asking *you* out," Tom said.

"You're not?" Danny grinned. "Don't break my heart."

"I'll leave that to Isabella." Tom picked up his notebook and crossed out SEAFOOD from his list. Then he noticed that Danny looked somber. "What's the matter?" he asked.

"Sometimes this whole relationship thing scares me," Danny said. "I mean, look where you and I were at the beginning of the semester.

We were scared to death of commitment. Now we're both in love, man. Things have changed fast with us. Real fast, and they could change back just as fast."

"Yeah, I know." Tom frowned. He did know. But knowing Elizabeth had convinced him that love was worth the risk.

Danny was looking at him with his eyebrows raised.

"We've put all that behind us," Tom said firmly. "Most of it was just rotten luck."

"If you say so, Tombo." Danny shook his head. "I guess you don't believe in jinxes or evil spirits."

Someone knocked on the door, and Tom opened it. "It's the beautiful and talented Ms. Ricci," he announced. "Come on down!"

"Hi, guys," Isabella said. She wore a black jumpsuit, three silver bangles on one wrist, and long, flashy earrings. Although Isabella wasn't exactly his type, Tom thought she looked great.

Isabella walked over to Danny, flung her slender arms around his neck, and kissed him on the mouth. Tom cleared his throat and looked at the ceiling.

"OK, OK." Isabella slipped away from Danny and sat on the edge of his desk. "So what are you guys up to tonight?"

"Nothing much," Danny said, "now that you're sitting way over there."

113

"Work and studying," Tom said. "Do you have a better idea?"

"Oh, I'm sure I could think of something," Isabella said, smiling at Danny.

"Well, I guess I'll just head over to the station." Tom stood. *Might as well leave the love-birds alone,* he thought. Besides, he did have work to do.

"What's the next news sensation?" Danny asked.

"Something on how wealth corrupts, specifically boy-millionaire Bruce Patman," Tom said, searching for his notebooks under the clutter on his desk. "I have a source who says that he now buys the answers to most of his exams. He also gets a little extra help writing his papers."

"The opposite story would be one on how the ex-jocks feel about losing their scholarships," Danny said. "You've got to hurt a little for them— it's tough to pay the bills without a scholarship."

"Well, we figured out how," Tom pointed out. "And what do you know—we got *academic* scholarships. It turns out membership in jock-dom isn't the only reason to go to college."

"Most of those jocks were crooks," Isabella agreed, yawning.

"This is why I'm not a jock anymore," Danny said. "Their problems put beautiful girls to sleep."

"I'll leave you to devise a way to wake her up,

114

Daniel. Catch you later, guys." Tom grabbed his jacket. Once outside, though, he headed for Elizabeth's dorm rather than the TV station.

He knew she was at the library, but he wanted her to know she was in his thoughts. He tore out a page from his notebook and wrote:

Your beauty calls to mind every rose I ever saw,
The soft flicker of every candle,
The mysterious spell of every forest.
                    I love you.
                    Tom

He folded the paper in half and slid it under her door. He owed her a love note. After all, their one-week anniversary was only two days away and he had never written her one.

"Do you like to play outside?" Celine asked Matt. She had run into him in the hall of their building, apparently by chance. In reality, she had spent an hour chain-smoking by the door and listening for him.

"Sometimes," Matt said mockingly. "If my mother remembers to put on my galoshes."

"No, no," Celine said, shaking her head impatiently. "The saxophone. How about an outdoor concert some morning?"

Matt looked at her more closely. "I'm not an early riser. I play off-key until noon. Why?"

Celine smiled. Somehow, a fringe benefit of her plot to get Elizabeth was that she said extremely strange things, and Matt seemed to find them fascinating.

"I want to give my friend a birthday surprise," Celine explained. "She wakes up at six with the twittering little birds, wondering what to do with herself."

"Have what's-his-face who gets up with the flies serenade her."

"He doesn't play an instrument," Celine said, drumming her fingers on the wall.

"So do it a cappella." Matt yawned and stretched. Celine could see this was going nowhere. She was getting annoyed with him, and not just because he refused to help her. He really seemed bent on staying loyal to that chick at Swarthmore, even when he had a gorgeous girl within arm's reach.

Now I'm not just losing out to real girls; I've got competition from asinine pictures taken in a photo booth, she thought. Celine had seen a picture of Matt's angel on his dresser yesterday when she'd invited herself in for bagels. That was apparently all he ate: plain, pumpernickel, egg, and cinnamon-raisin bagels. He ate them bare, nothing on them, toasted black. Then he washed them down with murky espresso he cranked out in a portable pot. Celine shuddered at the memory.

Celine narrowed her eyes as she watched Matt put the key in his lock. Funny, now that she thought about it, the girl in the picture had looked a lot like Elizabeth—same blond hair, bohemian vest, stupid, earnest expression. *Well, well.*

"How about a little something to eat before you start tootling?" Celine asked sweetly. She could feel an idea dawning. Wouldn't it be a riot to make Matt think Elizabeth liked him, get him chasing after her, and bust him up with his girl-friend? Elizabeth, of course, would never go for him—she was too in love with Tom Sir Galahad Watts. But the whole thing *would* annoy her. Especially when she found out who was behind it. And, in the end, Matt might realize that he had the wrong taste in women all along and turn to Celine for comfort. Perfect. She could take him or leave him. "I have bagels," she added.

"Why not?" he said, stepping into her apartment.

Celine smiled. Maybe the princess would get her concert after all.

Mike screamed. Literally howled, like a starved coyote. "Turn the friggin' TV back on!" he yelled.

Steven shook his head. "You're not watching *Fort Apache* for the two hundredth time. Not unless you get over there and turn it on yourself."

Mike fell silent. Steven turned to leave the room and measure out Mike's painkillers. Until the caretakers were sure Mike wouldn't commit suicide, they were locking the pills in the bathroom cabinet.

Suddenly a glass whizzed by Steven's head. It soaked his ear with cold water and smashed into the bookcase.

Steven could feel a slow rage start. *Talk about gratitude,* he thought. *Why in hell does Mike blame me for his every last frustration?* The crippling shot had been fired by Mike's gun, not his. Mike had been trying to *kill* him, for God's sake.

Steven closed his eyes and began counting to ten. At seven he heard Mike's voice, coming at him in nasty spurts.

"It's no wonder you get off tormenting me," Mike was saying. "If I lived with an ugly, dumb woman, I might look for cheap thrills like taunting an invalid too."

With difficulty Steven sucked in air. *I am going to get a dustpan and broom,* he told himself. *They are in the kitchen. I will not pay attention to anything else that happens on the way there.*

"I never could figure out what made you so crazy about me and Jess," Mike continued calmly. "Was I getting more of it than you? Is

118

that it, Wakefield?" Suddenly Mike sounded vicious. "You hypocritical, snot-faced idiot—"

Steven couldn't take it. Not when it was about Billie. He lunged for Mike.

Mike tried to lift his weak right arm to protect himself, but his arm fell. A bewildered, helpless look spread over his face.

Steven stared at Mike's thin body, bent at an odd angle on the couch. Steven knew he must have a snarl on his face like a wild animal's.

Abruptly he dropped his hands. Pity and guilt drowned out all his anger. He felt exhausted. Without saying anything, he walked slowly to the kitchen and fetched a broom and dustpan. Then he began to sweep up the broken glass, hearing Billie's voice in his mind.

"You spent months staring out the front window of our apartment," Billie had said to him on the phone that morning. "You wouldn't talk to me or look at me. How do you think that made me feel? Steven, I *loved* you."

That might have made him feel better, if it hadn't been in the past tense.

"Will you get me my pain medication?" Mike said neutrally.

"Yes." Steven stopped sweeping and went into the bathroom to measure it out. His hands were still shaking. He returned to the living room and handed Mike the pills and small plastic cups. Then he picked up the broom again.

119

Mike had it wrong: Steven had been the ugly, dumb person living in his apartment. Maybe he should call Billie tonight and tell her that.

"I don't live with her anymore," he said into the silence.

"Sorry," Mike said flatly.

Steven stopped sweeping. For a moment he thought he had heard real sympathy in Mike's voice. But he must have been mistaken.

Chapter
Eight

"Here's the church, here's the steeple; open the door and see all the people," Jessica said on Thursday afternoon, leading Lila up the steps of Theta house. Isabella had invited them over for a quick tour. Jessica had already shown Lila her dorm room and treated her to an espresso at the coffeehouse.

They'd had an emotional reunion, hugging, kissing, and crying. Then they'd looked each other over. To Jessica's relief, the only sign of Lila's recent troubles was her fashionable black skirt and blouse, accented with an expensive-looking silk scarf. She had half expected Lila to be gaunt and muffled in a veil.

Lila stopped at the bottom of the steps to the sorority. "We always thought we'd be Thetas together," she said wistfully.

"Maybe we still can be," Jessica said. She felt

more energetic since Lila had arrived, as though she now had a powerful ally—or at least an ally.

Lila opened the front door and walked into the spacious hallway. "Very, very nice," she murmured. "Original Victorian doors and wall paneling . . ."

Jessica could hear the sounds of an argument from the second floor. The fight seemed to be advancing toward the staircase. "Oh, absolutely!" Alison Quinn's voice trumpeted. "A divorcée and a widow—that will really add class to our house!"

A moment later Isabella hurried down the stairs, looking unhappy. Alison glided after her. She didn't look surprised to see Jessica and Lila.

Jessica flushed.

"I think I've seen enough," Lila said coldly, eyeing Alison.

"Hi, you guys," Isabella said, making an apologetic face behind Alison's back. Jessica felt a little sorry for her. Obviously Alison was out to embarrass all three of them.

Alison walked to the front door, then suddenly whirled around. "Lila Fowler! That *is* you! You just look so different . . . so . . . mature. Where *have* you been keeping yourself?"

She seemed about to go on, but Lila cut her off. "Here and there, Alison," she said. "How is everything at home?"

Alison's eyes widened for just a second.

"Oh—just fine; same as always," she said quickly.

"Sorry we can't stay." Lila began pushing Jessica toward the door. "We've got appointments."

At the end of the front walk, Lila finally stopped pushing Jessica. "What was that all about?" Jessica asked. "You already know Alison?"

Lila shrugged. "Alison and I go way back; our families have known each other forever. That's why I was surprised when you said she's in line to be president of the Thetas—I guess for once her reputation hasn't preceded her."

"What do you mean?" Jessica asked eagerly, hoping to hear some delicious dirt about Alison. She herself had certainly supplied Alison with enough food for fun over the past few weeks.

"Al's a klepto," Lila said, raising a hand to shade her eyes from the setting sun. "Two years ago she went into Asterid's dress shop in L.A. and tried to rip off a thousand-dollar dress. Of course, a place like that has security coming out the kazoo, and she got caught. What she did was entirely stupid—I think she must just not have been able to stop herself. For a while things looked really bad: the store was threatening to prosecute, and they would have won the case, obviously—there was Alison, with the stolen dress in her sticky little hand. She could have wound up in reform school. I guess her parents gave the store a whopping bribe to drop the charges and shut up about what happened. They must have shut everyone else up too—sounds like only the immediate circle heard about it, which includes the Fowlers."

Jessica stood with her mouth hanging open. This was juicy dirt indeed.

"So," Lila said, tossing her long dark hair over her shoulder. "Let's get out of here, before we run into Alison again. What are you going to show me next?"

"Bruce Patman." Jessica pointed down the sidewalk. "Or at least he's going to show himself. A live exhibit from Sweet Valley High."

"Great," Lila muttered. "I knew something was missing in my day."

"Who's the guy with him?" Jessica asked, peering into the winter sunlight slanting through the trees.

Suddenly she knew. He had bright blue eyes under thick black hair, and he was tall: she remembered that from the way he had to duck under the fire-exit sign to leave the classroom. It was the gorgeous premed from chemistry. The one who looked like James Bond.

He was talking earnestly to Bruce as they approached. Jessica had never seen him smile, but then, chemistry had never made her smile either. Of course he would be the serious type, since he was headed for medical school. She wondered what those soft, sensuous lips would look like laughing, or kissing . . .

"Lila!" Bruce called. "Welcome back." He seemed genuinely glad to see her. "And there's my favorite Jessica," he added.

"How many Jessicas do you have?" James Bond asked.

I knew his smile would look like that, Jessica thought. *Warm, with that little-boy sparkle.* She smiled back.

"I'm James Montgomery," he said. "You're in my chemistry class, right? Welcome to the world of reagents."

"Jessica Wakefield," Jessica said, laughing. She put out her hand. He took it between both of his, held it a couple of seconds, then released it.

"Sorry I didn't introduce myself before," he said. "But I've been kind of overwhelmed since the beginning of the semester. I'm on the soccer team, so I spend most of my life at practice or in the weight room." He didn't sound as though he minded. "Then I've got my duties of Sigma treasurer. And I'm a premed, headed for a brilliant career as a surgeon. Or so my mother hopes."

Well, what do I say to that? Jessica wondered. *My paralyzed husband and being permanently behind in classes aren't very good conversation openers.*

"Girls make lame pilots," Bruce was saying loudly to Lila. "I never knew one who could even remember to put the wheels down for landing. Did you know that's the most common cause of crash landings with amateur pilots? It's all those women in the air."

Lila was looking at Bruce with real annoyance. "I'm an excellent pilot," she said coldly.

It occurred to Jessica that she really should jump into this conversation before Lila and Bruce started hitting each other. They had never gotten along in high school. That was mostly, Jessica thought, because they were so alike.

"My plane's a beautiful baby," Bruce went on enthusiastically, ignoring Lila's angry glare. "A Cessna 310. It really claws the sky. James, my man—maybe we'll take her out sometime."

Lila tossed her hair over her shoulders again and said nothing.

Bruce stopped talking and stared at her. "Do you really fly? Where?"

"In Italy, with my husband," Lila informed him loftily.

Bruce whistled. "That's right—I heard you were married. Your husband's a brave man to let you take up his plane."

Lila gulped and for a second seemed to lose her composure. "He *was* a brave man," she said softly. "He died."

Bruce and James stared at her in horror.

"Sorry," James said, backing away.

"We're really sorry," Bruce said, giving her a

pitying look. "Jeez . . . I didn't . . . Well—we'll talk to you guys later."

The two men walked quickly off, bumping into each other in their hurry to leave. Jessica might have laughed at their butchering of the situation if Lila hadn't looked so crushed.

"Lila?" she said, touching her friend's shoulder. In the swiftly falling darkness she couldn't make out Lila's expression.

"It's all right," Lila said. "Somehow I knew my social life here would get off to a real bang-up start."

"Bryan finally spoke to me today," Nina told Elizabeth. "I guess we're on OK terms for now."

Elizabeth had caught up to Nina in her dorm room. Nina had been hiding in the stacks for most of the past thirty-six hours, trying to think things through and figure out where she had made mistakes. No one had found her—she had been on the top floor of the library with hundred-year-old legal documents, inhaling dust.

"So what did he say?" Elizabeth asked.

"I guess I did most of the talking," Nina said. "I ran into him after class yesterday afternoon, but I could see he was just going to walk by." Nina took a breath. "I promised to go to the next BSU meeting. Then I apologized about fifty times for missing the last one."

"Hmmm," said Elizabeth. "That might encourage him to act like a jerk again."

"Well, if the meeting is so important to him, and *he's* so important to me, I want to be there," Nina said, looking at her fingers. "The causes they're fighting for are really important, Elizabeth."

"I realize that and I agree with you. But he's got to try to be more understanding of what you want," Elizabeth pointed out.

"Oh, I know. But what happened after we fought was kind of overwhelming." Nina glanced at her friend's concerned, attentive face and felt a little better. "I got scared. It wasn't just Bryan who wouldn't talk to me. . . ."

"Who else?" Elizabeth pressed. She searched through her knapsack and brought out a granola bar. Breaking it down the middle, she gave half to Nina and put her feet up on the bed.

Nina ate the granola bar. She didn't say anything.

"Go ahead," Elizabeth said gently. "You know I won't tell anyone."

"It's more I don't know if you can understand." Nina looked at the ceiling. "None of the other BSU members would talk to me either. I was being boycotted."

"Really?" Elizabeth looked startled. She was silent for a few seconds. "Well, I suppose that kind of thing happens," she finally said. "I mean, the Thetas boycotted Jessica for weeks. I guess they're still boycotting me, come to think of it," she added. "I don't care."

"But I *do* care, Elizabeth," Nina said. "I care a lot. I know what the BSU is doing is necessary—they're really standing up against racism on this campus. I admire people who are politically active; it's just I don't have a lot of time for activism right now. I wish I was smart enough to be an activist and still study as much as I need to." Nina smiled wryly. "Bryan isn't going to like that attitude, is he?"

"Probably not." Elizabeth's blue-green eyes seemed darker than usual. "But, Nina, you have to make yourself happy. You have to do what you think is right. It's as simple as that."

Nina sighed and slid her hands along her jeans. "I know."

"You've seen their point; maybe they'll see yours and stop hounding you," Elizabeth said encouragingly.

But Nina shook her head, clicking the colorful beads on her braids. "I don't think so," she said slowly. "Elizabeth, yesterday, before I apologized to Bryan, I ran into one of the BSU guys at the snack bar. He looked right through me as if I didn't exist. I don't want to risk becoming an outcast again. I'm not going to try to make my point in their face."

Elizabeth nodded, although she didn't look as though she completely agreed.

The next major trick, Nina thought, *now that everyone is speaking to me again, will be juggling my huge paper that's due next week with the march the BSU has planned for then.*

But somehow she would do it. She couldn't let Bryan down again.

I wonder which is more depressing—my room or this place? Jessica thought, looking around the library. In the carrel to her left was Todd, nervously chewing the eraser on his pencil. Just ahead of her, unbelievably, was Peter Wilbourne. And to her right was Alexandra Rollins, pretending to study but mostly sighing heavily and monotonously kicking her chair leg. About once every five minutes Peter would try to hit her up for some notes.

Nerd school, Jessica decided. *We're all nerds in training.* She was supposed to meet Elizabeth here for a sisterly cram session, but apparently Elizabeth had found something else to do.

"Todd!" someone whispered loudly. Jessica looked around and saw Lauren Hill hurrying through the new-books section.

Todd's head was bent over his book. He was keeping his place with one hand and rubbing the back of his neck with the other.

"What are you doing?" Lauren asked, not bothering to whisper.

"What does it look like, Lauren?" Todd finally looked up. "Do you think I'm playing basketball?"

"Shh!" Jessica said. Peter joined her.

There was a pause. Jessica read a sentence in her history book. She'd had so much practice studying lately, she was almost getting good at it. To her surprise, sometimes she even liked it. It was a frightening concept.

"We need to talk," Lauren said to Todd.

Jessica looked over again. Lauren was trying to sound calm, but her lip was trembling and she was almost in tears.

Todd turned back to his book. "I've got to study," he said. "I have a big test tomorrow."

Jessica read a little more. Then Todd's books flew to the floor with a crash.

"You can't do this!" Lauren screamed. "You can't just dump me and avoid me! Who do you think you are?"

"Lauren, not *here*," Todd said irritably. "What is your problem? We broke up, all right? Deal with it."

"I can't stand this anymore." Lauren wiped away her tears. "Please, Todd. I just need to be with you for a little while."

Todd stared at her contemptuously. Then he stood and strode out of the library, leaving his books.

Instantly Lauren turned and ran after him. Jessica could hear their voices as they left the library, arguing loudly.

I know somebody who's sorry he dropped Elizabeth, Jessica thought. *The more Lauren chases Todd, the harder he's going to run from her.*

"Poor Lauren," she said to Alex.

"Yeah," Alex answered tonelessly.

Jessica gathered her books. Definitely her room would be less depressing.

"Jess! Wait!" Elizabeth hurried through the stacks, dropping papers, then picking them up. Despite her irritation with Elizabeth for standing her up, Jessica had to admit that her sister looked wonderful. She was thin and practically glowing with happiness.

As Elizabeth tried to reorganize her pile of books, one of them fell onto Jessica's desk.

"Lord Byron," Jessica said, reading the cover. "Are we sending a little love poem to someone we know?"

"No, no." Elizabeth was still trying to catch her breath. She sat down in Todd's empty chair. "I've got to prepare a poetry reading. I put a yellow sticky on the one I chose."

Jessica turned to the page and began to read aloud.

> "They name thee before me,
> A knell to mine ear;

132

A shudder comes o'er me—
Why wert thou so dear?
They know not I knew thee,
Who knew thee too well:—
Long, long shall I rue thee,
Too deeply to tell . . ."

Jessica looked up and realized her sister was paying absolutely no attention to her. Suddenly she realized why. Tom was making his way through the biography stacks. "Well, here he is at last," Jessica said. "Dream Man. I didn't think I could live for another second without him."

"Tom!" Elizabeth called.

"Oh, Tom! Over here!" Jessica wailed in a falsetto.

"Stop it, Jess." Elizabeth frowned at her twin.

"How can I stop, Liz?" Jessica screeched, forgetting to keep her voice down. "My heart is about to burst out of my bosom!"

"I mean it," Elizabeth warned.

"I mean it too," Jessica said. She knitted her brows and pursed her lips in an exact imitation of her sister.

Tom rushed over to Elizabeth and they kissed. Jessica suffered in silence for a while. Finally she made a sucking noise. They ignored her.

"All right, listen up!" she suddenly yelled.

Tom and Elizabeth came unstuck slowly. They stared at her.

"I'm going back to the room," Jessica said firmly. "Liz, I want you to recite one line of poetry for me before I go."

Of course, with Tom around, Elizabeth only got through a couple of words before she either forgot where she was or started giggling.

Jessica hastily packed up her books and papers. "See you later, guys," she said.

"Yeah, later." Elizabeth didn't take her eyes off Tom.

"See you, Jessica," Tom said politely. At least he still came out of the twilight zone sometimes.

Elizabeth really should get herself together, Jessica thought as she hurried out of the library. *Before this personality change becomes permanent.*

Chapter Nine

"Winnie, you're hurting my hand," Denise said, trying to yank it away.

"I'm not letting go of it," Winston told her, with more confidence than he had felt in days. "Not until five after eight Saturday night, when Bruce will serve your dinner to someone else because you're late."

Nobody else in the coffeehouse took the slightest notice of the struggle going on under their noses. But then, he and Denise came in here a lot and people were probably used to them. Winston smiled. He liked that thought.

Denise rolled her eyes. "I can't drink my coffee," she said. "It's on that side. Hold my other hand for a while."

Winston switched. "Are you ready for your big date with Bruce?" he asked.

"I have never been so thrilled," Denise said,

sticking a finger in her mouth and gagging. "Win, how many times do I have to tell you that it's not a date? Like I would date him. Like I'd waste a whole evening on Bruce Mr. Ego Patman if I didn't have to. Jeez, Winnie, there's no way I would do that even if you weren't sitting on my hand, having kittens."

"You're mixing your metaphors," Elizabeth said gaily, coming up behind them with Tom.

"No, I don't think I am," Denise said, looking at where her fingers disappeared under Winston's legs. "There's no other way to describe this guy. At this rate he's not going to live to turn forty. So, how are things with you, Elizabeth?"

Thirty, Winston thought sullenly. *Possibly twenty.*

"Oh—just great!" Elizabeth said airily. "Are these chairs taken?"

"Nope," said Denise. "Except I think the ghost of Bruce Patman is sitting in one."

"Very funny," Winston grumbled. "Hey, Elizabeth, do you think Bruce has gotten even more stuck-up than he was in high school?"

Elizabeth didn't answer. She was busy laughing at some private joke with Tom.

"Young love," Winston explained to Denise, as Tom leaned over to kiss Elizabeth. Winston sat back and shook his head. He had never seen Elizabeth like this, and it made him uneasy. He had the feeling that love had made all of them go a little nuts.

"We may do a story on Bruce," Elizabeth said, coming up to breathe from Tom's kiss. "About what it's like to go from—well, I guess in his case, from rich to richer."

"That's pretty dull," Tom said, laughing.

"Oh, no—everyone's obsessed with Bruce," Winston said. "Trust me."

William lay on his bed, smoking, his eyes on the ceiling. Time crawled by. Finally he looked at the door. Strange sounds floated through it: the snarls of an argument, probably over which TV channel to watch; a weird cackle; a distant wolf howl from the wacko in solitary confinement.

William inhaled sharply on his cigarette. This was the one place where you were still allowed to smoke inside.

The insane asylum.

They had ways of making you behave. Solitary confinement was one.

Not that he would mind being alone. But it might be harder to escape from there.

He had to be sure that no one knew about his plans. If they found out, they would drug him. Other patients had already shown him how to fake taking his "meds." If he caused any trouble, though, the orderlies would strap him down and inject the drugs. All for his own good, of course. To calm him down. To make him normal.

Well, they hadn't gotten to him yet. He was still perfectly sane. As brilliant as ever.

His thoughts drifted where they always did: to Elizabeth. "I'll find you," he whispered. "You're still with me."

He swung his legs over the side of the bed and sat up. Time for group therapy. He had no way of knowing exactly what time it was; the orderlies had taken his watch during the strip search when he was admitted into this place. The patients' personal belongings were taken to prevent theft or, William supposed, to prevent suicide by watch scratching. But William knew that stripping the patients of everything they had was just another way to humiliate them. Humiliated people were easier to control.

William strolled toward the locked, barred door that separated the dangerous patients like himself from the more manageable ones. On the way, he smacked into a young man who thought he was a bird. The poor guy flew around the ward all day and night, cooing. William shoved him viciously into the wall.

In the large communal room, most of the inmates were lounging on the floor, watching TV. They looked insane. That was because of their clothes, which were about a hundred different shades of red and yellow polyester. Some strange charity had donated the clothes to the poor patients.

William had been allowed to keep his own clothes, but last night a crazy bank robber had ripped William's elegant suit coat almost in two. That had happened during a poker game in which the robber had accused William of cheating. William *had* been cheating, but the assault had enraged him anyway. He had barely been able to stop himself from . . . taking appropriate action.

But drawing attention to himself didn't fit in with his plans.

He had been able to repair his coat with clumsy stitches. But he had exacted a small revenge: he kept his winnings from the poker game, which were the robber's entire supply of cigarettes.

Keeping an eye out for his enemy, William backed up against the locked door. In a few minutes an orderly would come through the door to collect the few D-ward patients who could behave themselves well enough for group therapy. Most of the group was made up of patients from the temporary ward.

Today two murderers waited patiently with William for the key to turn. One of them had attacked and robbed elderly men who reminded him of his father, and the other had gunned down the three boyfriends of his unfaithful wife.

The murderers looked peaceable enough, at least for the moment.

The orderly arrived and let them out, counting. It wasn't the usual orderly. It was a student intern, a young woman. She still got misty-eyed when she saw the miserable human beings in the D ward. The men liked her, and most of them tried to be nice to her. William smiled at her sadly and walked through the hall with his head down.

He went to group therapy because it was part of cooperating. The psychiatrists got angry with anyone who didn't go to group, although they denied it.

The arts and crafts room was as cheery as a kindergarten. William lounged in a chair near the door.

"Mr. Miller!" rapped the psychiatrist who had admitted William to the institution. "Please proceed. Last time, I believe, we were discussing exactly why you killed your wife's second boyfriend."

Most of the faces in the room were frozen in sadness. Mr. Miller blubbered away about the boyfriend, who had watched his favorite movies from Mr. Miller's easy chair.

William smiled contemptuously. His mind began to drift into that twilight where Elizabeth appeared: her smile, her hand in his, her lips trembling under the impassioned touch of his own. He had never given so much of himself to anyone. All the things she'd said. What had she said . . .

Mr. Miller threw a basket of paints. William ignored the chaos that resulted. Pulling out a felt marker, he turned to a clean page in the notebook sitting on a table next to him.

He was above this stain of humanity. He had a letter to write. She was waiting.

Celine carefully taped the flyer to Elizabeth's door, then tiptoed down the hall.

Matt had been a bit skeptical at first when Celine told him that Elizabeth Wakefield was wildly in love with him.

"Why?" he wanted to know. "Who is she? She doesn't have a clue who I am."

"She's heard you play in—the football band," Celine guessed, hoping Matt was one of those dorks in straw boaters who kept the spirit alive at the games. "Saxophone music is really her thing. She won't stop asking me about you."

"Oh." Matt had gotten a smug look on his handsome face, and then they'd gone off looking for Elizabeth. Matt wanted to make sure that she would do as an admirer. Celine had stationed them at the north end of the quad, where they had a good view of the paths criss-crossing the college.

"Whoops! There she goes again," said

Celine, pointing at Jessica. "That girl certainly does get around."

Matt looked confused. Celine had discovered that away from his music stand, he was a lost soul.

But after he had seen two Jessicas and one Elizabeth, he had willingly given her a handful of posters for the concert and permission to tell Elizabeth that he was starring.

"Celine?" a sharp, suspicious voice echoed down the hall.

Oh, this is all I need, Celine thought irritably. *Elizabeth again, after I spent the whole afternoon on her.* Celine didn't see her that much now that they weren't roomies, but she sometimes had the distinct sense that Elizabeth was haunting her.

With Elizabeth was none other than Tom Watts, Man of the Year. He had ignored Celine, then pretended to date her, and finally just stood by and watched while she was handcuffed and carted off to jail after that infernal Sigma episode.

"Well, if it isn't my favorite two reporters," she drawled, stopping near the staircase in case she needed an escape hatch. "How are Lois and Clark?"

"What are you doing in the dorm?" Elizabeth asked in the same nasty voice.

"I used to live here . . ." Celine said, pretending to be mortally hurt. "I'm seeing my friends."

"What friends?" Tom asked, sounding just like Elizabeth. They might as well be an old married couple.

"You," Celine said immediately. "I just couldn't pass up the chance to talk over old times."

"Oh, right," Elizabeth said, rolling her eyes. "Give me a break, Celine."

Celine turned and fled. "I don't want to talk to her anyway," she muttered, grabbing both banisters as she raced down the stairs. She had had enough of Princess Priss to last a couple of lifetimes.

"Now what?" Tom asked Elizabeth.

"I can't believe how fast she went down those stairs in two-inch heels," Elizabeth said thoughtfully. Suddenly she saw the poster. "Why is that there?" she asked, pointing.

"I don't know." Tom leaned closer to read it, brushing her cheek with his fingers. "Hey, Charlie Parker. Do you want to go? The soloist must be pretty good to tackle Parker's tunes."

"Sure," Elizabeth agreed. *Good, clean fun,* she thought. *Not sexy fun, lots of other people around.* She was beginning to be a little nervous about where all her dates with Tom seemed to end up: alone with each other, usually kissing passionately on cots, beds, and floors.

That could lead to only one thing. Sometimes Elizabeth thought she was ready for it. But then, she had been sure a couple of times with Todd, too. Now she was glad she'd waited. Sleeping with someone for the first time was a decision she wanted to make with her head, not with her body.

"Anniversary night," Tom said, "is the day after tomorrow." He caught her hands and brought them to his lips, closing his eyes as he bent to kiss them. Then his eyes met hers. "I want us to have a very special time," he whispered.

Elizabeth looked at him intently. She'd seen Tom's face with so many different expressions in the past. When they had worked on news stories together, his forehead was furrowed with concentration and his eyes glittered with excitement. Otherwise, he had kept his face guarded and closed.

Now Tom's face was openly loving. Elizabeth's heart began to beat faster. "What have you got planned?" she whispered, letting him pull her close.

"A lot." Tom put his lips to her hair. "But for Saturday night . . . tell me how this sounds. We'll start off with Mexican food at Gurulés'; you know, where the strolling troubadours serenade your table. Then we'll take a drive for dessert, to a wild, secluded place I know. I want to be alone with you on a mountaintop and tell the sky how I feel about you."

Abruptly Jessica swung open the door to the room. Tom and Elizabeth fell in, giggling. When Elizabeth straightened up, Jessica was scowling at them and tapping her foot.

Like an old schoolmarm, Elizabeth thought, trying to choke back her laughter. *Is that how I used to look? No wonder Jess was always bugging me to lighten up.*

"Mañana," Tom said softly. He touched his lips to her cheek. With a sigh, Elizabeth watched him go, relishing the look of his broad shoulders and his confident walk. Her hand lingered on the spot he had kissed.

"He's with you every minute of the day and night," Jessica muttered, marching back to her desk. She cleared her throat noisily. Then she tossed Elizabeth's poetry book at her, hitting the back of her leg.

"Hey, don't break the spine!" Elizabeth said indignantly, retrieving Byron from the floor. "I get the message."

The book opened itself almost magically to her poem. Another note fell out. The black, bold letters said, *I need you.*

On Friday morning Lila dropped the spoon into her uneaten cereal and pushed back her

145

chair. Her mother looked at her expectantly.

"So today's your first class," Mrs. Fowler said. "What is it?"

"Psychology 105. Human behavior."

Her mother seemed to be waiting for her to say more. "Will you excuse me?" Lila asked politely. Mrs. Fowler had been hovering over Lila like she was an abandoned puppy ever since she had gotten home. She appreciated the attention, but it was getting a bit stifling.

Maybe it's time I moved to the dorms, she thought, heading upstairs to her bedroom. She knew she wasn't really ready for the party scene or the questions people would ask. On the other hand, staying at home made her feel isolated, and someday she was going to have to get used to telling people about Tisiano.

Lila threw open the doors of her enormous walk-in closet. It was time to decide what to wear to her first day of college. Normally her closet would be bulging with clothes. But now it was empty except for a skimpy collection of black things: a few plain dresses, a skirt and blouse. The only shoes left were black flats. The day she'd arrived home, Lila had yanked everything out of the closet and told Rosa, the Fowlers' housekeeper, to give it all to charity. Now she wondered if Rosa had. Probably not—she would have had to hire a truck.

Lila wondered how much face she would lose

if she asked Rosa for her clothes back. Seeing Alison, Bruce, and that new guy yesterday had reminded her of how important appearances were. Then again, she could buy a whole new wardrobe if she wanted. The widow of Count di Mondicci was even richer than Lila Fowler had ever been. A whole new wardrobe full of color.

Wasn't wearing black the same as wearing her broken heart on her sleeve for everyone to see?

Lila stepped into the closet and ran her hand lightly along the bar. Empty hangers rattled like skeletons.

Then, to her astonishment, she saw something swaying gently at the far end of the closet. Looking more closely, she saw a navy SVU sweatshirt, a short denim skirt, and a hand-tooled-leather belt. On the floor were new sandals. Pinned to the sweatshirt was a note that said *To our college girl. Love, Mom and Dad.*

Lila smiled and kissed the note. Then she quickly slipped into the new clothes and examined herself in the mirror.

A college girl, ready for fun, stared back at her. The stately, glamorous Countess di Mondicci seemed to have disappeared. Lila stared at herself, a bit unnerved.

Then she reached into her jewelry box and took out the last present Tisiano had given her, the diamond necklace. She held it to her lips for a long moment and closed her eyes against the tears. She fastened it around her neck.

Diamonds with a sweatshirt probably looked weird. But she wanted to carry a little of Tisiano into her new life.

After a last admiring look in the mirror, Lila skipped down the stairs and ran into the breakfast room. Mrs. Fowler was still reading the paper, her hand absently groping for her coffee. Lila flung her arms around her from behind. "Thanks, Mom!"

Her mother turned. "Oh, sweetheart! You look just beautiful. I think I'm almost as excited about college as you are."

Lila smiled and held back another wave of tears. "I should be back for dinner," she said.

"Have a wonderful time," Mrs. Fowler called to her as Lila hurried off.

Lila drove to SVU a little faster than the speed limit allowed. When she reached the university grounds, she parked and went straight to her psychology classroom, which Jessica had pointed out the day before.

As she entered the room, she saw Bruce Patman giving a speech to a crowd of guys. "I'll take up any Sigma brother who wants to fly," he said loudly.

"Small planes are dangerous, aren't they?" one of his admirers asked.

"Not if you're a world-class flier," Bruce boasted. "Hey, Lila!" He actually stopped talking long enough to wave at her.

Lila gave him a small smile and sat down. Bruce was gorgeous, even *she* had to admit that, and the fact that he knew it had always made him intolerable. She opened her textbook, surprised at how much Bruce's bragging annoyed her. It wasn't like it was anything new.

Bruce had always been obnoxious about his family's money. Obviously getting access to his trust fund had just made him worse. But Lila knew that Bruce thought *she* was the one who was crass. Apparently this was because the Patmans were an old-money family, while Lila's parents had made their fortune themselves.

"I'm not the one who flies a stupid mass-produced Cessna," Lila muttered. She and Tisiano had owned a beautiful custom-made plane.

The professor came in, ending Bruce's lecture. Lila took careful notes as the professor talked. Even though she wasn't taking the class for credit, she was ready to be serious about her education.

After class she reviewed her notes while the other students stampeded for the door.

"Lila!" Bruce made his way toward her through the rows of desks.

"Yes?" Lila began to put away her books.

"I wanted to tell you again, I'm sorry about what happened. I know how you feel," Bruce said, his voice somber.

149

Lila looked at him in surprise. This didn't sound like the Bruce she knew. Could he possibly have become a human being while she was away?

"I know how hard it is to lose someone you love," he went on. "I went through that with Regina Morrow in high school, remember?"

Lila couldn't help but remember—Bruce's girlfriend had died of a cocaine overdose and it had rocked the entire school. It had been horrible, but still, it wasn't like losing a husband. She stood up angrily and stalked off without a word.

"Listen, why don't I take you for a ride in my plane sometime!" Bruce shouted after her.

In your dreams, Lila thought, practically running to her car. She sat there for several minutes, her hand on her forehead, trying to let go of some of her anger.

As she relaxed a little, the red-tile buildings of the university dissolved. In her mind she saw a gleaming red-and-orange plane, flying from the blue horizon, the faint buzz of its engines breaking the perfect quiet of the sky.

Chapter
Ten

"It's the catapult principle," Danny told Isabella, squinting at his fork loaded with refried beans. It was targeted on Tom's head.

"Never mind," she replied. "He doesn't see you."

"I see him," Tom said calmly, although he was alertly watching Elizabeth. "If that fork fires, you're going to be wearing this taco as a hat, Daniel, my friend."

"Have you noticed that guys never seem to outgrow their food-throwing years?" Isabella asked Elizabeth.

"Ummm . . . yeah," Elizabeth replied.

She seems a little distracted, Tom thought. She was staring grimly at her cheese sandwich, which she had stripped of its olives, dressing, and ham.

"I would never throw a taco at you," he said.

Elizabeth rewarded him with a brief smile. Then she pushed back her chair. "I've got to find Jess. We were supposed to go shopping an hour ago."

Tom caught Elizabeth's hand and pulled her to him. "I know something's wrong," he said. He had to find out what, right now, even if Danny and Isabella were openly smirking at them.

"Oh—" She didn't meet his eyes. "It's just . . ."

"What?" Tom prompted. Just that dissected cheese sandwiches were depressing? Or that she'd woken up this morning and decided she didn't love him anymore?

"I think I've put off seeing Todd as long as I can," she said. Now she looked at him, with that steady, crystal-clear gaze that always went straight to his heart. "He left me four messages last night. But I really don't want to see him. He'll just make another scene. And he's . . ." She hesitated.

"Drinking," Tom finished.

"Well . . . yeah," she said.

Tom sighed irritably. He wished Todd would find something to do besides bother Elizabeth.

"Why are you wasting time on that jerk?" he asked. "Tell him to take a perpetual hike."

"I will," Elizabeth said, standing up. "I'll call him now." She slung her backpack over her shoulder. "I'm just not sure he's going to accept it."

"Try to see him today, if you have to," Tom said grudgingly. "Tomorrow's our anniversary. I don't want to see him, hear him, or know he's alive tomorrow."

Elizabeth smiled at him radiantly, the clouds vanishing from her blue-green eyes. "It's going to be the best anniversary celebration ever," she said, putting her lips to his cheek. "I can hardly wait."

"I'm so sorry, Jess," Elizabeth gasped, rushing into their room. She had left the cafeteria with some attempt at dignity, then run to her room like a six-year-old, with her arms, legs, and hair flapping. Never mind Todd; she had to get to the mall. He would just have to be patient a little longer, or she wouldn't have anything decent to wear to her anniversary dinner. "Do you still have time to shop?" she asked her sister.

Jessica, sitting over the open Byron book, held up a finger. "Let me finish."

Elizabeth sat obediently on her bed while Jessica recited the poem that Elizabeth had chosen for the Literary Club meeting tomorrow night. It was hard to believe that Jessica, California's number-one party girl, had just told her to shut up for a poetry performance. What was most astonishing to Elizabeth, though, was that her sister was reciting from memory and not looking at the book at all. She recited with beautiful conviction.

Elizabeth applauded at the end. "Now if I can just get it down half as well for the reading tomorrow night—" At that moment a terrible, impossible thought struck her. "Oh no! NO!"

Lila took a white sweatshirt with navy lettering from a wire bin at the campus bookstore and put it on top of her other purchases. For a moment she traced the SVU insignia on one of the notebooks she had picked out. She had gone for a drive, enjoying the fresh air on her face, until her anger at Bruce had died down to just her usual annoyance with him. He wasn't worth worrying about.

Lila took down a navy-and-white pompom from a shelf and shook it experimentally. Maybe she would try out for cheerleading next semester.

"Doing a little shopping?" asked an acid voice.

Lila put down the pompom and turned to face Alison Quinn. "Yes, I am," she said pleasantly. "Just some school supplies."

"I have all that stuff already," Alison said, waving her hand. "In triplicate."

I'll just bet you do, Lila thought. *And I'll bet you stole half of it.* She said out loud, "How are things at Theta house? I'm so sorry I had to run off yesterday, but"—she shrugged gracefully—"I had some crucial appointments to keep. Jessica has told me a lot about the Thetas since I got back."

"Jessica Wakefield," Alison said. The corners of her mouth turned down. "She has the manners of a lumberjack."

"Does she," Lila said, gritting her teeth. She didn't feel like humoring Alison. But she also didn't want Alison as an enemy, opposing her pledge. The game would be interesting.

"I wonder how Jessica's divorce is coming along," Alison said casually. She was examining Lila's outfit. Lila priced Alison's suede shoes at about three hundred fifty, Ruby's, San Francisco.

"Annulment," Lila corrected. "It's supposed to be final any day now."

"We Thetas help battered women through charity; we don't take them into our sorority as members," Alison commented. "It's barely possible that we might—and I emphasize *might*—take the unusual step of repledging Jessica. After all, her mother is a very influential alumna. That's really the main reason we might rethink our decision. But I'm against it, and I've got company." Alison stopped speaking and casually leaned closer to Lila.

"Just a word of advice to an old friend," she continued, her voice sugary. "It is *not* a good idea for you to be perceived as Jessica's friend. You don't want to be lumped with the sad cases."

"Oh, no; of course not," Lila agreed. She

and Alison stared at each other meaningfully for a few seconds.

Finally Alison said, "Good. I think we understand each other." With a nod, she turned and walked out of the bookstore.

"We certainly do," Lila murmured.

"What's the matter?" Jessica asked Elizabeth, watching her sister's face fall.

Elizabeth put her hand to her forehead. "I just realized the poetry reading is tomorrow—"

"Yeah? Big deal," Jessica interrupted.

"It *is* a big deal!" Elizabeth wailed miserably. "Tomorrow night is Tom's and my . . . it's our . . ." She looked at Jessica sheepishly. "It's our one-week anniversary. He planned a big night out. I can't miss it." She collapsed on her bed. "But I can't flunk English either, can I?"

Jessica shook her head.

"Tom will kill me if we don't go out after all the plans he's made," Elizabeth moaned. "I'm already in trouble with him because Todd won't leave me alone."

"Tsk, tsk," said Jessica.

"What am I supposed to do?" Elizabeth demanded, frantically running around the room. "I can't be two places at once—"

Suddenly she stopped short and stared at Jessica. "Hey, wait a second."

"Oh, no, you don't," Jessica said, burying her nose in a book.

Elizabeth snatched the book away. "Please, Jessica. Please, please, pretty please do my poetry recital for me," she begged. *"Please?"*

Jessica got up and stood by the window. She folded her arms across her chest.

"Aren't you the girl who wouldn't kiss Peter Wilbourne when your sister's whole social life at SVU depended on it?" Jessica scowled at her, obviously enjoying herself.

"This is for the sake of art," Elizabeth said feebly.

"It took art to kiss Peter and not barf at the same time," Jessica reminded her.

"Please, Jess?"

Jessica drummed her fingers on the windowsill.

"What if I—what if I . . . bought you a new dress at the mall?" Elizabeth asked in a rush.

"Two," Jessica said immediately.

"Don't be ridiculous!" Elizabeth protested.

"You're the one who has money in your bank account," Jessica said sweetly.

Elizabeth grimaced. She always had more money in her bank account than her sister—because she didn't waste it. "All right, let's go shop," she said, grabbing her jacket. *I'd better get her attention on clothes racks as soon as possible,* she thought. *Before she has me walking on my hands for the rest of the semester.*

"Throw in a new spring wardrobe and I might entertain Todd for you too," Jessica suggested. She made a face. "No, scratch that. He's too depressing these days."

"Tell me about it," Elizabeth said grumpily.

Jessica stopped at the door and turned. "But seriously, Liz, what makes you think I can do a poetry reading?"

Elizabeth stared at her. "You were just doing it. That was as inspired a reading as I could give." *Certainly now, when I can't seem to concentrate on anything,* she thought. "Don't sell yourself short," she finished.

"OK," Jessica said, grinning. "So we have a deal. Two new dresses. How about being my maid for the rest of the semester too? Put away my clothes, make the bed, polish the mirror. You know how messy I am."

"This is blackmail," Elizabeth moaned.

"In fact," Jessica said cheerfully, "why don't you pick up a little now, before we go?"

"One is sort of California casual—you know, a beach-type dress, very short, with a bold blue-and-white pattern, and the other is basic and black," Jessica said over the phone to Lila. The two new dresses Elizabeth had bought her that evening hung frontways in the closet so that she could keep on admiring them—and so that Elizabeth could too.

Jessica glanced at them to check the accuracy of the details she was relaying. "They were Elizabeth's treat," she said, smiling as she remembered the shopping spree. Elizabeth had actually almost thrown herself on the floor in Jessica's path at one point to stop her from making a beeline to the most exclusive store in the mall. The beach dress had lived there.

"Why would she do that?" Lila asked disbelievingly.

"She's just really glad I'm her sister," Jessica said fondly.

Lila snorted.

"She needs me," Jessica said sentimentally. "I'm doing a poetry reading for her tomorrow night so that she can gush away the hours with Tom. She's in my power."

"Poor Liz." Lila laughed. "I really feel for her. So what are you doing tonight? Anything exciting?"

"Not really," Jessica said. "I'm going to a jazz concert at the coffeehouse in a few minutes. I need to get away from my chemistry book for a couple of hours, and I don't want to be by myself and . . . think. About, you know, Mike. That whole deal."

"Is he any better?" Lila asked neutrally.

"I don't think so. Steven says he's a little better physically, but Mike just . . . hates everyone. I don't know if he'll ever get over that. You're almost lucky your husband died, Lila—" Jessica stopped herself with an embarrassed laugh. "I don't really mean that, Lila. I really don't. I just meant it's hard when—"

"Never mind," Lila cut her off abruptly. "So who are you going to the concert with? Liz?" she asked in a lighter voice after a moment's pause.

"No, alone," Jessica said, feeling the strain in their conversation. "I'm going to sit as far away from Liz as possible," she said. "I can't stand another minute of her and Tom. I'll be in the front row, under the stage lights."

"Sounds fun. Wait, I called to tell you I had a run-in with the Queen of Mean tonight before I left campus," said Lila. "Our own Alison Quinn."

"Oh, her." Jessica yawned and lay back on her bed.

"She said some pretty nasty things about you, Jess," Lila said. "She kind of said that she wouldn't oppose my pledge, but she's going to take an active role against you."

"Yeah, I know. I don't think there's any way I can change that." Jessica couldn't even imagine what it would take for her to suck up to Alison at this point.

"You never know," Lila said thoughtfully. "Maybe there is."

*   *   *

Lila sank into her soft, pillow-laden bed and ran her hands through her hair. *How could Jessica tell me I'm lucky Tisiano died?* she thought. *I guess no one will ever understand what that part of my life was like. It really is just memories now.*

Lila went over to the window and peered out between the curtains. The stars looked like tiny frosted cookies in the hazy night. Here in her parents' house, after a day spent with her old friends, Italy and Tisiano seemed almost unreal even to her.

The roar of a Jaguar's powerful engine shattered the stillness. The Jag swung into the driveway and parked. Her father was home from Italy.

Just as well he broke the mood, Lila thought, backing away from the window. *I can't stand here all night, thinking of the past.* Lila opened her bedroom door to go down and greet her father. Then the pale-blue phone on her nightstand purred.

Lila picked it up and sat on her bed. "Hello?" She hoped it was someone she liked. She still couldn't shake the dark mood that had set in when she saw Bruce that morning.

"Lila—how are you," said Bruce's voice.

She dropped back onto her pillows. "What a coincidence, Bruce," Lila said calmly. "I was just thinking about you."

"How about that," Bruce said, apparently not hearing the irony in Lila's voice. "Great minds think alike."

Lila smiled slightly. She had never had a problem with Bruce's ego. Lila thought well of herself too.

"Listen, I called because I want to take you up flying," he said. "The world looks beautiful from the sky, and your problems seem a lot smaller."

Lila frowned. What was this? Bruce wanted to go on a date? They hated each other. "Why do you want me to go flying with you?" she asked, not bothering to sound particularly nice.

"To do you a favor," he said.

"Some favor," Lila said.

"Are you scared to fly?" he asked. "You said you flew in Italy."

"Are you saying I didn't?" she asked stiffly. Bad enough that Italy was starting to seem unreal to her, without Bruce implying she had made up the whole thing.

"Don't be so touchy," he said with a laugh. "All I meant was, did you ever really *fly*—over tough terrain, do acrobatics."

"No, Bruce, I can't say that I have." Lila stood and began to pace the room. "The Italian Alps are just little molehills compared to what you must have flown over. Any puddle jumper could do the Alps with one propeller out. And the acrobatics that we used to perform at some of Italy's largest air shows I'm sure wouldn't have impressed you at all."

"You flew acrobatics?" Bruce asked, sounding amazed.

"Sometimes," Lila said nonchalantly. She didn't want to carry her bragging too far. That would be reducing herself to his level.

"Wait—let me get this straight—you're saying *you* flew acrobatics. Not your husband, but you yourself."

"Yes." Lila wedged the phone between her cheek and her shoulder and picked up a nail file.

"We should definitely fly together," Bruce said. "Although I don't think I'm going to let a girl at the controls of my plane, acrobat or not," he added insultingly.

"Suit yourself." Lila put down the nail file and began hunting under the bed for her pair of Nikes.

"Don't be so sensitive," Bruce said, sounding annoyed. He obviously didn't like being turned down. "Flying would get your mind off your problems."

"I'll think about it," Lila said, to get rid of him. She couldn't imagine being shut in a cockpit with Bruce, listening to him brag nonstop for hours. If she needed to escape, ten thousand feet was a very long parachute ride.

*   *   *

Elizabeth walked down the aisle of the cozy, candlelit coffeehouse holding Tom's hand and searching for good seats. She stopped a few tables from the front, made her way to a seat, and turned to face him.

"Tom, we've got to . . . give it a rest for a little while," she said once he was seated beside her. "I don't want to, and I know *you* don't want to, but I'm having trouble concentrating on anything."

"You're not breaking up with me, are you?" Tom turned pale.

"Of course not!" Elizabeth cried, squeezing his hand. "I just have to figure out how I got into this mess with Jessica." At that very moment Elizabeth saw Jessica walk in from a side door, take a front seat, and open her program. Jessica was wearing her new black dress.

Then the door burst open again and, to Elizabeth's amazement, Celine paraded across the coffee shop. She took a place a table down from Jessica in the front row, and put her feet up on the stage.

What on earth is Celine doing here? Elizabeth thought distractedly. *Are jazz concerts part of her academic probation?*

Elizabeth leaned over to Tom and they kissed. And kissed again. The lights dimmed.

"Can you push over, Watts?" Todd whispered loudly.

Elizabeth broke apart the kiss, stifling a gasp with her hand.

Tom twisted around and stared at him.

"Or should I walk over your chair?" Todd asked, sounding dangerous.

"Come on, Tom," Elizabeth said quickly. Tom moved over next to her. Their arms bumped, and Elizabeth's program slid down her leg. They both grabbed for it at the same instant.

"Sorry," they both said at the same time.

They returned their hands to their laps.

The sweet smell of bourbon drifted to Elizabeth's nose. Looking over, she saw Todd furtively put a mini bottle to his lips. Elizabeth faced front and tried to ignore him. The band began to play.

Nice music, Elizabeth thought. Tom was beating his hand on the table, either to keep time with the music or from suppressed rage.

Elizabeth stole a look around him at Todd. Todd was sitting perfectly upright. Occasionally his head would jerk forward as if he were falling asleep.

Maybe he's too drunk to do whatever he planned to do when he sat with us, Elizabeth hoped. *How am I going to handle this?* She knew Tom was about out of patience with Todd.

The band began a light, graceful number. Elizabeth sighed miserably. She felt as if her life was getting out of control.

Then another voice in her head spoke up. It didn't care what was out of control as long as Tom loved her and she loved him.

Things aren't quite so simple, the first voice interrupted. *You're getting in real trouble. Todd and Tom want to kill each other. If you don't do something, they probably will. And if you keep forgetting school assignments, you're going to have to keep asking Jessica for help. Just remember, no one can afford to dress Jessica permanently.*

Todd jerked up his head and muttered something. Elizabeth glanced over in alarm, but he seemed to nod off again.

Tom fidgeted. Maybe the smell of the bourbon was bothering him, too. In the dark, she couldn't tell if he was on the verge of meltdown or not. Elizabeth tried to pay attention to the concert, but the music had stopped.

The lead saxophonist stood, tucking his horn under his arm. Elizabeth noticed vaguely that he had dark hair and a quirky, rather attractive smile. He pointed at Jessica and said, "I'd like to dedicate the next song to Elizabeth Wakefield, the prettiest saxophone fan on campus."

"What?" Elizabeth cried.

"What?" Jessica yelled from the front row.

Celine whistled.

Todd stood up and applauded.

Chapter Eleven

I can't recite a poem in front of a roomful of people, Jessica said to herself as she pushed through the student union door. A crowd of faculty and students, all wearing tweeds and intellectual expressions, greeted her. It was Elizabeth's crowd, waiting to hear profound verse.

Jessica looked down at the brown corduroy pants, tan wool sweater, and simple gold locket she had on. *I can't suffer through wearing Liz's clothes for an entire evening either,* she thought.

"Ah, Ms. Wakefield." An attractive man with horn-rimmed glasses held up a hand in greeting. This must be Elizabeth's adored Professor Martin. Jessica was beginning to understand why she liked him so much. "You will read Byron third, after Shelley and Keats go off. We are looking forward to it."

"So am I," Jessica said unconvincingly, fiddling with the barrette that held her hair back. Before she'd left her room, she had tried to make herself presentable with a good dose of blush, but of course Elizabeth wouldn't let her.

"At least there is absolutely no chance anyone I know will be here," Jessica murmured. "If I trip walking up there, or forget my lines, no one will ever know except Liz's pointy-headed friends. And she can't make me take the dresses back because I already wore the black one."

The first reciter was a bushy-browed guy in a red beret. He scowled at the audience as he sat down on the stool placed at the front of the room. Then he whipped his beret dramatically over his heart and began to recite loudly.

Spare me, Jessica thought. The poem was very long. Jessica thought about where to debut her new beach dress.

The audience clapped politely at the end of the poem. Jessica clapped too, choking back a nervous giggle. *Please don't let me think this is funny,* she begged herself. *I'm right in the front—I can't sit here and laugh hysterically without people noticing.*

The next reciter strode to the stool. She was an athletic-looking woman in her thirties, wearing a windbreaker, corduroy pants, and hiking boots. Jessica looked down at the hiking boots she herself was wearing, and winced. Good old Elizabeth.

The woman smiled at the audience. Then she stepped forward dramatically and bellowed, "Ode to a Nightingale!"

Jessica shrank back. The woman practically leaped across the room. "My heart aches, and a drowsy numbness pains/My sense, as though of hemlock I had drunk!" she shouted, flipping up an imaginary cup.

Elizabeth didn't say anything about acting out the poem, Jessica thought, caught somewhere between laughter and worry. *Is that what I'm supposed to do?*

The woman hurled herself at the audience, still reciting. Jessica hastily pulled back her feet. Finally the woman looked upward, an anguished expression on her face, and the poem was over.

Despite her fears, Jessica couldn't stop another giggle. She rummaged in her purse for a handkerchief to hide her face until she got herself together. The woman was still staring at the ceiling. Finally Professor Martin got up and half helped, half pushed her back into the audience.

"Our next poem will be Lord Byron's 'When We Two Parted,'" he announced.

Swallowing hard, Jessica walked to the front and sat on the stool.

"Elizabeth Wakefield," said the professor. "One of our journalism students."

The audience was quiet and expectant. Jessica stared down at her hands in her lap, trying to still the hammering of her heart. At last she looked up—right into James Montgomery's sapphire-blue eyes. For a moment the world seemed locked in stillness as they stared at each other.

"Ms. Wakefield?" Professor Martin prompted.

Jessica sat up straighter and cleared her throat. Suddenly she knew just how this poem should be said. It was a simple story of a love that was over, a love that might have been saved if the poet had really understood the other person.

> "Thy vows are all broken,
> And light is thy fame:
> I hear thy name spoken,
> And share in its shame."

Jessica recited steadily. She could feel tears starting in her eyes. This was for Mike, the man she'd thought she wanted to be with always. This was for their love that had burned itself out like a falling star. The poem flowed from her, as if it were part of her.

> "If I should meet thee
> After long years,

How should I greet thee?
With silence and tears."

Jessica finished. Slowly, she bowed her head. The applause roared in her ears.

Startled, Jessica looked up. James was beaming at her and clapping enthusiastically.

A dark figure stood in front of Mike's door. Steven's heart soared. Billie!

He walked slowly up to her. "Hi."

"Hi," she said, looking at him with an uncertain smile. "I brought you some dinner, since you're going to be stuck here so late with Mike. Your favorite—Chinese. I got Mike the same. He can have it, can't he?"

"Yes," Steven said, taking the bag of food. "Thank you." For some reason, as overjoyed as he was to see her, he felt no particular need to talk. She hadn't said much either when he called her last night. She'd listened to his apology and thanked him, then said she'd think things over.

Steven put a hand up to her silky hair and cupped her cheek. She laid her hand over his.

Billie's eyes were shining. "See you later," she whispered.

Steven watched her disappear down the stairs. He stayed by the door for a minute. "At home?" he asked. It wasn't much more than a whisper.

She turned around slowly. "Yeah. At home."

He stood there, letting the blessed knowledge that she hadn't given up on him soak through his mind. He had missed her so many nights this week. He couldn't sleep without her.

Tears filled his eyes. He blinked them away and opened Mike's door.

Mike wasn't in the living room, and the TV was off. Steven ducked into the bedroom. No Mike buried under covers on the bed. Amazing.

Steven found him in the kitchen, reading a magazine. Mike had pulled his wheelchair up to the table, and the overhead lights were on. He had dressed himself in jeans and a clean black T-shirt and combed his hair.

Well, well, Steven thought. *Don't tell me we've decided to rejoin the human race.* On closer inspection he saw that Mike was reading a motorcycle-parts magazine.

"The night nurse called in sick, so I brought dinner," Steven said, thumping the bag on the table.

"What?" Mike asked, not looking up.

"Chinese." Steven got out plates and forks and poured two glasses of soda.

"Beer," Mike grunted.

"You're not supposed to have alcohol," Steven said firmly.

Mike didn't answer. He began to eat the roast pork lo mein with gusto, mastering the chopsticks that had come with the meal. Steven was surprised—it looked as if Mike was recovering a little motor coordination.

Now's a good time to push forward with the rehab, Steven thought. *He's physically well enough. I don't care if he hates me for it: tonight I'll force him to do everything for himself. Otherwise I'll be trapped here forever.*

After they finished eating, Mike turned to Steven. "I gotta go to the bathroom," he said, casting an eye over his magazine again.

Steven hesitated. "I'm not going to take you."

"What do you mean?" Mike asked angrily. "That's your job."

"Do it yourself," Steven said calmly. "I know you can."

Mike turned the wheelchair around and sat, waiting for Steven to push him. Steven shook his head, forcing Mike to look up to catch his response. Mike's eyes were clear and seemed completely focused. He needed only half the pain medication he had at the beginning of the week.

Then, to Steven's surprise, Mike began raving like a maniac. He was so wild, Steven could barely understand a word. *Why is he going completely crazy now when he's finally getting better?* Steven wondered.

"You do what I tell you to!" Mike shouted. "After what you've done to me! You ought to be on your knees, begging for forgiveness, instead of screwing around with me!"

Furious, Steven opened his mouth to rage back. The urge to hurt Mike, at least with words, was even stronger than usual—Mike was better now. He could take it.

But Mike was still in a wheelchair, where Steven had helped put him, permanently. That was the unavoidable fact. Steven closed his eyes and slowly let his anger die away. When he opened them, Mike was weeping bitterly into his hands.

"Maybe I should work on my looks," Winston said to himself, examining his face over the sink in the bathroom mirror. "While I wait for Denise to come back from her big date with Patman."

The key to staying sane tonight, Winston had decided, was to instill a little order into his life. When he had first come to college, he had had a lot of plans for self-improvement. True, some of them had fallen through. When he had pledged the Sigmas, the brothers had tried to murder him. And the women in his dorm had put a wrench in his idea of developing a really stupendous physique by borrowing all his weights.

But still, all wasn't lost. Unless Denise spent the night with Bruce.

Winston clenched his teeth and forced his mind back to his plans. He took his Ray-Bans from the shelf and put them on. "Now, who has my weights?" he said aloud.

"Don't ask me," said Anoushka, one of his hallmates, pushing through the bathroom door with a bucketful of shower supplies. "I press real weights over at the gym."

After living for three months among two hundred women with strong personalities and limbs, Winston had learned not to respond to such remarks with something like, "Go curl your hair." "You haven't seen my weights?" he asked cautiously.

"I saw the five-pound ones." She dumped her bucket next to the shower. "I'll tell you where if you'll tell me why you're wearing sunglasses at night in the bathroom."

"You wouldn't understand," Winston said, snatching them off.

"I bet I wouldn't," Anoushka agreed. "Can I persuade you to go to your room or outside? I want to take a shower."

"Where are my weights?" Winston demanded.

"Debbie had them the last time I saw them, but that was Monday," Anoushka said, leaning thoughtfully against the shower divider. "Someone else probably has them by now. You'll just have to go bang on doors until you find them. It will give you something to do while Denise is at Sigma house."

Winston groaned. He should have known that everyone on the hall would be thoroughly briefed about his problems. "I don't want to see anyone," he mumbled. "They'll just pity me."

"Winnie, you've got to be nuts to think that Denise would fool around with Bruce." Anoushka clapped her tropical fruit shampoo and cream rinse on the tile shower floor.

"Of course she wouldn't," Winston said. "Just because he's rich, has a body like Arnold Schwarzenegger, and flies around in his own plane is no reason for a girl to go out with a guy."

"He doesn't have anything between his ears," Anoushka said with exaggerated patience. "And he's an egomaniac. Look, why don't you go lie down in your room with a cold compress on your forehead? Or watch horror movies. You like that, don't you?"

"I can't watch horror movies without Denise," Winston said childishly. "She tells me when I can look."

Maia pushed open the bathroom door.

"Winnie's in crisis about Denise," Anoushka told her without preamble.

"Read a book," Maia said, setting her case of steam curlers on the shelf. "Something really brainless that will give you a good laugh."

"Thank you, ladies," Winston said, backing toward the door. "You've given me a lot to think about."

But once he had escaped to the safety of his room, Winston found that being alone was worse than listening to the advice of his hallmates. Much worse.

He began to pace with his hands behind his back. "Where is she!" he cried. He was insane. He knew exactly where Denise was, of course. At Sigma house, in Bruce Patman's room. In his arms, no doubt.

By nine o'clock Winston had blisters from walking so many miles around his room. He stuck Band-Aids to the hurt places on his feet, changed shoes, and went outside.

Other students were hurrying back from the library, from the coffeehouse, and from other night spots. Winston saw Elizabeth's friend Nina Harper, her pretty face puckered in a frown, passing under the trees toward her dorm. He wondered if Nina's problem could possibly be as hopelessly depressing as his—he doubted it. Winston flung himself down on a bench in front of the shadowy biology building to rest his blisters.

Suddenly a dark shape sprang at him from behind a bush. Winston stifled a shout when he realized it was Todd.

"Hey, Todd," he said, trying to appear composed.

"Win, I need to talk to somebody," Todd said thickly, dropping on the bench beside him and laying a heavy arm around Winston's shoulders.

"No, you don't," Winston said, trying to wrestle free. "You need a pot of black coffee, a cold shower, and Elizabeth Wakefield."

At the mention of Elizabeth, Todd groaned and leaned even harder on Winston's shoulders.

"Todd, please," Winston said, trying to move away from Todd's breath and his misery. "I have enough to worry about right now. Find somebody else to spill to."

"I can't." Todd sighed and flopped his head back, looking at the sky. "I can't go any farther. I feel like this is the end of the road, you know?" He shook Winston's shoulders.

"Yeah, I kind of do," Winston said, trying to make his teeth stop rattling.

"Where's Elizabeth? She didn't meet me tonight. Nobody answers the phone. She broke a promise . . . my heart, I guess . . . When I trusted her . . ." Todd seemed to lose his train of thought.

Oh, man, Winston thought dismally. Todd hardly seemed to know who he was talking to. Any pair of ears would do.

"She's with him," Todd went on, choking.

178

"They're together. I can feel it. God, what if they . . ."

But Winston was gone.

After two Shakespeares, another Byron, a Berryman, and a bunch of poets Jessica couldn't remember had gone by, the poetry recital was over. Jessica stood and shook her hair back over her shoulders. She sighed. There was no point in hanging around here, since she didn't know anybody. James had disappeared right after the last poem. She probably shouldn't stick around anyway—someone might ask her difficult Elizabeth questions about oxymorons or something.

Jessica paused at the door, wondering where to go. Well, of course she could study. Jessica grimaced. She wasn't sure she could face another night of being completely alone, knowing there was no chance her studying would be interrupted by noise, laughter, or fun. Elizabeth was out on her dream date with Tom, and the room would be too quiet.

I guess I could study in the coffeehouse, Jessica thought, pushing through the door into the warm night. But that would be worse. Someone might walk up and laugh in her face as she sat there dateless on a Saturday night.

Back to the room, Jessica decided. Elizabeth might turn up. Although she'd spend hours discussing all the gory details of her romantic evening. Or maybe, even more depressing, Elizabeth wouldn't be back at all tonight.

Jessica took off Elizabeth's jewelry and stuffed it in her pants pocket. At least she could get out of these clothes and put on something presentable. She began walking back to the dorms, cutting behind the student center. Then she heard heavy, quick footsteps behind her.

Jessica had been jumpy about walking alone at night since she had been attacked one night by some secret society goons. Instinctively she whirled to face whoever it was, and found herself looking into the distinctive blue eyes and handsome face of James Montgomery.

"Tell me just one thing," he said.

Anything, Jessica thought. *Just so long as you keep looking at me like I'm the one and only girl in your life.* "What?" she said, smiling.

"Why are you pretending to be Elizabeth?" he asked.

Jessica had forgotten she had been. "Are you sure I'm not?" she teased. There was no way Jessica was going to let this hunk escape just to save Elizabeth's face.

James took her hands. "Believe me, I'm sure it's you," he said. "Elizabeth doesn't have this effect on my heart rate."

Jessica blushed at the obvious sincerity of the

compliment. *It's amazing he knows I'm not Liz,* she thought. *Especially since I didn't majorly screw up the poem.* Very few people had ever been able to tell the twins apart when they switched clothes.

"Do you like poetry?" she asked. Apparently he did, but she was surprised and a little impressed. She would have expected to find a premed in a laboratory cutting up dead animals, not at a poetry recital.

Obviously James had a wide range of interests and was sensitive. *There's a Liz thought,* Jessica said to herself, grinning. *Maybe it's rubbing off of her clothes.*

"Of course I like poetry," he said. "Especially when a beautiful woman recites it with such emotion."

Jessica's spirits fell a little. She remembered whom she had been thinking about while she recited. "I guess the poem has some personal meaning," she said.

James continued to gaze at her admiringly in the yellowish light from a streetlamp. "You worked hard tonight to bring that poem to life," he said. "How about if I reward you with an espresso and a chocolate croissant at the coffeehouse?"

Jessica hesitated. This sounded like a date, or at least a good time. She wasn't allowed to have good times. Not when Mike was a cripple and studying was the most important thing in her life.

Then she imagined her dark, still little room, tidied to perfection by Elizabeth the Clean, and the stacks of books teetering on her desk. Virtue had its limits.

"I'd love that," she said, permitting herself just one Jessica Wakefield guy-killer smile.

I don't need to feel guilty over a little cup of coffee, she thought as she happily followed James along the path to the coffeehouse. *It's not like I won't go back to studying and feeling miserable about Mike right afterward.*

Elizabeth put her glass to her lips and smiled at Tom.

"Happy anniversary," she said softly.

Tom sat across the picnic blanket from her, watching her in the light from a gold candelabra. A black-forest cake with two slices missing sat in the middle of the blanket. Tom's dark eyes traveled slowly over Elizabeth's hair to her clothes, his gaze deeply admiring.

Elizabeth knew she looked beautiful. She wore a blue suede skirt and vest that brought out the ocean blue in her eyes. Her blond hair flowed down her back, gathered into a turquoise-and-silver clip.

The wind rattled the pine needles in the trees above. Elizabeth looked up. The trees grew so thick in the forest that only a little moonlight filtered through the branches. She was glad that after a delicious Mexican dinner they had driven here, far along a dirt trail, where they could be absolutely alone.

Tom took her shoulders in his hands. "Happy anniversary," he whispered huskily, and then his mouth found hers. His hands moved gently from her hair to her face, as if he couldn't stop touching her. "Are you mine?" he whispered.

"All yours," she reassured him, looking up into his adoring face. *This is such a miracle,* she thought. *He really does love me.* For so long she had wondered if he ever would. Tom lowered her to the ground and they began to kiss, gently at first, then more passionately.

A heavy raindrop plopped onto Elizabeth's face. She reluctantly pulled away from Tom and sat up. The mood was broken. *It's probably a good thing,* she realized, coming down from the land of spinning trees, sexy male cologne, and a wish to keep going.

Tom kissed her forehead. "Let's pack up. We don't want you to melt."

"I don't think I'm that sweet." Elizabeth tried to gather her hair back into its clip. "The cake is, though."

They threw the picnic stuff into the back of the Jeep and climbed in. Tom backed it cautiously around, then drove slowly along the dirt road. The headlights made a tunnel under the black trees.

"So what's next?" Elizabeth asked, yawning. She was glad she had driven up so that Tom was driving back.

"Dancing," he said. "Tom's place."

"Sounds good," Elizabeth said, yawning even more hugely. "Then it's back to the real world, I guess." She slid across the seat and snuggled against him. She wanted to catch a couple of Z's before they got home and went back to celebrating. As she watched the trees go by she felt her exhaustion settle over her like a thick blanket.

She had Celine to thank for that. At six in the morning Elizabeth had woken to the sounds of a saxophone playing "When Irish Eyes Are Smiling." Elizabeth hadn't been able to find out why the mysterious saxophonist had dedicated the song to her at the concert the night before. But this morning, he had been playing under her window, and Celine was with him. Elizabeth still didn't know exactly what was going on, but now she knew who was behind the plot, whatever it was.

Elizabeth felt herself drifting off to sleep. She was thinking of poetry, of the perfect poem about her relationship with Tom.

"Thanks for those love notes you left me," she

murmured. "They were a really nice surprise."

"I left you only one," Tom told her.

"Mmmmm," Elizabeth said sleepily.

A three-quarter moon was rising, illuminating the waving arms of the trees, the cracked cement of the sidewalks, and Sigma house. Winston stared with a determined expression at Bruce Patman's second-story window.

"I'm going up," he muttered.

A group of Sigmas turned onto the path to the house. "Hey, Egbert!" one of them called. "Just can't stay away from us, can you? How about walking a windowsill tonight?" They all laughed as they headed to the door.

Winston marched after them, barely registering the taunts. "I have to go in," he muttered. "I have to get her."

He stood just inside the door for a second, getting his bearings. At the top of the staircase was Bruce's room. Somebody grabbed him by the scruff of the jacket and lugged him outside, flipping him upside-down as they went.

Winston had never understood before why men sometimes beat other men to a pulp. But at that moment he would have liked to pulp the person bumping him down the stairs on his head. The only problem with starting a fight was that the Sigma brother holding him weighed about two hundred and seventy pounds. Winston watched in numb fascination as a large German shepherd barked furiously at the brother's feet and Winston's head.

The brother dumped him on the path. Winston stood up, dusted off gravel, and made a dash at the door. He was beginning to think of this as a holy quest.

The guy was waiting for him and threw him out again. This time he tossed Winston into a hedge. The German shepherd bounded into the hedge with him. Winston looked up, expecting to be mauled into something unrecognizable, but the shepherd merely sat down beside him and licked his ear.

Winston sat in the bushes with his new friend, hugging the dog and trying very hard not to cry. Then he brushed off his pants and crawled out.

"Denise!" he shouted. "Denise!"

Silence. Winston had no idea what to do now except die of anguish. Then the door to Sigma house opened and Bruce came out, laughing. Denise was behind him, obviously embarrassed.

"God, Winnie, what is the matter with you?" Denise stared at him incredulously. "What have you been doing?"

Winston looked down at himself. Twigs, leaves, and other bush shrapnel stuck to his sweater, and he could feel streaks of mud drying on his face.

"Take care of this guy," Bruce said, still laughing. "He's always been hyper. Catch you tomorrow, Denise." He walked off.

Denise turned to Winston. Winston opened his mouth.

"Don't say a word to me, Winnie," Denise warned. "I don't want to hear a word."

"Leave them in her room, with the tops open," Celine instructed. "Won't she laugh when she sees flies all over her ceiling?"

Paul rolled his eyes. "I don't know about this," he said. "It's a corruption of the scientific method."

"Elizabeth is a girl with a real sense of humor," Celine insisted, shooing him out of her room with the rack of test tubes. "She'll laugh her pants off."

She practically had to push him out the door. Paul hadn't been too crazy about this scheme from the beginning. He had needed major coaxing to go along with it.

"What do you say to whoever opens the door?" Celine coached.

"If Jessica is there, I tell her I'm leaving the flies for a friend of Elizabeth's," Paul said with a sigh.

"Good," Celine purred. "If you have the rotten luck to meet Lizzie, throw the test tubes in the room and run—bombs away. But a few spies told me that lately she spends every night carousing with her honey, and her sister hangs out in the library. So probably you'll have to ask the dorm monitor to open their door. That will be easy; she can even stand there and watch you if she wants to make sure you don't steal the princess's prized pencil collection."

"I don't know." Paul's golden-brown eyes were unhappy. "What if whoever lets me in remembers me later?"

"It's not a crime to shoot off a few tubes of fruit flies," Celine said impatiently. "You're not going to let me down, are you?" she pouted, draping herself full length in the doorway.

Paul walked over to her, stood on tiptoe, and kissed her clumsily on the lips. "No," he said. "I'm just worried about my academic career."

Celine was a bit taken aback by his brazenness. Oh, well, she'd been kissed by worse.

"I wouldn't worry if I were you," she reassured him, hoping to get him on his way before he demanded more physical payment. Probably no one would notice him at all. Paul wasn't all that memorable.

He kissed her chin, which was the highest he could reach since Celine had on high heels. "I'll come by later," he said.

"Do," said Celine, slitting her eyes sexily. She could always manage to be out.

*　　*　　*

188

"All right, you win," Steven said with a sigh. "I'll take you." What was the use? He should accept his fate. Every day, for the rest of his life, he would be wheeling Mike's chair, lifting his heavy body, measuring prescriptions, and suffering verbal abuse.

And now it was almost eleven o'clock. The nursing service still hadn't sent over a substitute for the usual night nurse. Steven knew he'd be stuck with Mike until as late as midnight or even the next morning. He'd been refusing to take Mike to the bathroom for almost an hour, and Mike showed no signs of giving in.

"About time," Mike grumbled as Steven wheeled him into the bathroom. "Do you want to damage my kidneys along with everything else?"

Steven patiently, professionally assisted Mike in the bathroom. His own competence only depressed him further.

"How about getting yourself out of here?" he asked, almost pleading.

"No," Mike answered firmly. "I need help."

Despite his exhaustion, Steven noticed something different about this response: Mike was answering directly instead of grunting or swearing at him. They were almost having a real conversation.

Could it be a step forward? *Big whoop,* thought Steven. *He's progressing about as fast as the continents move.*

Without getting any argument or criticism, he brought Mike out of the bathroom and got him settled on the living room couch with *Stagecoach* and John Wayne. "I'm going to clean up the kitchen," he announced, even though he knew Mike wouldn't answer. What he really wanted to do was watch *Stagecoach* with Mike—they shared an appreciation for John Wayne, if nothing else.

He froze for a moment in the doorway to the kitchen. He thought he had heard Mike say "Thanks."

He swung around. "What? Did you say something?"

"No," Mike muttered.

Steven waited another moment, then shrugged. He walked back to the kitchen, opened a cabinet, and took out a can of cleanser. Methodically he scrubbed down the sink, then washed the dinner dishes.

I'm so tired, he thought, squeezing out the sponge. *I feel like I've been loading bricks all day.* Obviously the mental drain was the killer with this job. He tried to forget his exhaustion by thinking about the trade laws he had been studying this week in his international finance course.

All of a sudden Steven grabbed the edge of the sink, realizing he had almost blacked out. This was more than exhaustion with Mike. He had the symptoms of . . .

Steven looked woozily across the room at the stove. One of the gas dials was twisted on. The pilot light must be out, letting the gas escape unburned.

There must be a lot of gas in the room already if he felt like this. He had to get to the range to turn off the burner. Otherwise, he and Mike were going to die of gas poisoning, or even an explosion. As he tried to get his legs to move Steven thought how interesting it was that the gas had been left on. Mike must have been trying to cook something.

The extra dish that fell from Steven's hand as he dropped to the floor, losing consciousness— it meant Mike must have succeeded in cooking that something and eaten it. *What do you know?*

Chapter Twelve.

Later that night, Winston gripped his bouquet firmly in one hand and started down the hall toward Denise's door. Then he stopped, stuck his nose in the flowers, and inhaled deeply. He had just lost his nerve again.

"I need flowers that will make a statement of depression and wild optimism," he had told the salesgirl at the all-night florist. She had sized him up coolly, not batting an eye at his troubled appearance. Then she had quickly made up a bouquet of ten red roses, two black ones, and a halo of baby's breath. Perfect.

Winston got his feet in motion down the hall again. He had to see Denise. His need to find out if he was forgiven was getting stronger than his fear that she would slam the door in his face.

He knocked on her door. He knew she was there, because he had spent the last two hours

193

crouched in his room with his ear against the keyhole, listening for her lock to turn. Winston had stayed there since he got back from the florist, after Denise had ordered him home from Sigma house like a dog. Probably she was still furious.

Denise opened the door. Her beautiful face was expressionless.

Silently, Winston handed her the flowers. Denise took them. He put one foot forward to come inside. Denise shut the door on his toe. Winston stared at the blank face of the door, stricken.

Now what? he wondered. *Did she not see my toe? Is crushing my toe the answer to how she feels about me?*

"Denise!" he shrieked, pounding on the door. "Let me in! Please! At least tell me what you think of the black roses! Did you ever see any before?"

She opened the door again. "No," she said.

"No?" Winston asked entreatingly. He tried to read the thoughts behind that exquisite face. He couldn't.

"No, I've never seen black roses before—although they're stunning—and no, you can't come in," she said.

"Why not?" Winston begged.

"Because I've got company." Denise glanced over her shoulder.

Winston heard a male laugh in her room. Not even just in her room. From her bed.

What is going on here! someone screamed in Winston's head. *We have one fight, and she's got some guy in the sack a minute after she walks in the door with him?*

"Denise, you—" Winston slammed the door back against the doorstop. Denise caught it on the rebound, before it hit her.

"I what?" she demanded, staring at him coldly.

Winston's anger disappeared. This was too tragic to be angry about. He turned without another word and walked away.

Winston reached his room after what seemed like hours, let himself in, and shut the door. The sound had a dungeonlike finality. He leaned against the door and closed his eyes, letting the tears fall. Why had this happened to him? Denise had seemed to like him so much. To . . . love him. Obviously he hadn't understood at all.

Winston's knees began to wobble. He gripped the doorknob for support, but it suddenly twisted violently in his hand.

Denise barged into the room, whacking the door into the wall the same way he had in her room.

Winston's hand slipped off the doorknob. For a few seconds he felt like he was flying as he fell backward. Winston sat down hard in the middle of the carpet.

Denise marched over to him. "Come on, Winnie," she said, hauling him to his feet.

"Where are we going?" Winston asked weakly.

"My room."

"Why?"

"To talk."

Moments later Denise led him inside her room. The guy was gone, or he was hiding in the closet. Winston opened the closet. Jeans and shirts hung innocently in a neat row.

"I can't believe I have to tell you this," Denise said from behind him, "but the only thing that happened tonight with Bruce was that he yakked nonstop about his idiot airplane. I couldn't even get him to work on our project, the jerk."

"He thinks you'll do the work for him," Winston said. He was surprised his mind was working well enough to compose a sentence.

"Probably," Denise agreed. "Why don't you sit down?" She waved vaguely at the bed.

The minute I sit on that bed, the comparison begins, Winston thought. *Where did she put that guy?* He looked under the bed and pulled out his five-pound weights.

"Sorry—I meant to give those back to you," Denise said. "Or to Candy, actually; I think it's her turn. She thinks she's precellulite in the upper arms."

Winston slowly sank to the floor, his back to the wall.

"What is wrong with you?" Denise asked. She slid to the floor beside him.

"You know what," Winston muttered.

"No, I don't."

Winston couldn't resist anymore. He turned to look at her. Her soft lips were in a pout, imitating him. "That guy," he said. "Who was he?"

"I'll tell you if we can get off the floor," she said.

"Believe me, Denise, there's nothing I'd like better," Winston said. "I think my tailbone is broken. But I'm not getting on that bed when you were just on it with another guy."

"I'll have friends in my room anytime I want, Winston." Denise's lovely, clear blue eyes bored into his. "That guy was just a friend."

"Oh, sure—all my best friends of the opposite sex hang out on my bed with me too," Winston said, turning away. "Nothing to be upset about."

"We have to get something straight, Win." Denise was still giving him that look. "We're not going to have the kind of relationship where you're spying on me all the time and telling me what I can and can't do. You shouldn't be jealous. If you are, it's not my problem. I don't want you coming around to places like the frat house and embarrassing me."

Do you want me to sit around on my bed with other girls? Winston thought, but he didn't dare say it.

"We have to trust each other," she said.

"I'll remember that the next time I catch you on your bed with a guy," Winston muttered.

"I did that on purpose," Denise said. "I knew you'd be lying in wait for me, so I thought I'd give you something to see."

"Oh." Winston felt relief flash through him. But he still wouldn't look at her.

Denise rolled her eyes. "I want *you*, you idiot. Why can't you get that through your thick skull?"

Winston felt as though he were floating. Those were the sweetest, kindest, most romantic words he had ever heard.

Denise's face softened. "Do you really think I could just grab any guy and replace you?"

"Yes," Winston said, but he was looking at her now. "I love you," he blurted. "Please don't pull anything like that ever again."

"I love you too," said Denise. "But I'll pull anything I want."

She touched her lips softly, lingeringly to his cheek. Then she stood and flipped off the lights. "Let's work on your trust," she said.

William lounged in a solitary confinement cell. The bleak, pale light of the moon shone through the barred window that overlooked the grounds of the institution.

Two burly orderlies had thrown him in here yesterday when he had punched out three of the bank robber's teeth. The robber had been in the middle of a long, insulting description of William's mother.

William had agreed with the sentiment, although the remarks had been inaccurate: his mother was a drunk, not a prostitute. But the fight, and the punishment of automatic solitary confinement, had fit with his newest plans. So William had smashed the robber's face in.

He got up and looked between the bars of the window. The grim-looking window wasn't all that it seemed. Because of fire codes that some bleeding heart had written for the savages in solitary, the window opened with a key. And William had that key. He smiled and stretched, remembering the shadowy browns and greens of the forest yesterday, so welcome after the sterile white walls of his room. The sunshine had dappled the pine needles under his head as he had pulled Andrea, the student intern, to him for a very special kiss. Because he had been such a good boy, Andrea had taken him for a walk. She wasn't supposed to do that, but the resident psychiatrists had all been out of town at a meeting. The orderlies were happy to have one fewer patient underfoot so they could sleep better on the job.

William's smile twisted into one of contempt. Andrea was a stupid girl. She had actually believed William when he said she was beautiful. She even took the mental patients seriously when they raved about secret tunnels under the institution, where they said the psychiatrists took them for experimental treatments.

Andrea was right about one thing, though— William White didn't belong here with a bunch of lunatics. And so she had copied the key for the windows in the solitary confinement cells. He'd barely had to ask. After another session in the forest today, she'd retrieved his car keys for him as well.

William yawned, more to relax himself than because he was sleepy. He was wired. He imagined some of his thoughts flying on dream wings to Elizabeth, reaching her in her sleep. She must already know that he was coming.

Beautiful girl. Goddess. That pure, sculpted face, the perfect curve of her jaw, her soft lips, as exquisite as a flower. He would adorn her with jewelry and furs and cars; he would have her sit for portraits and statues. Soon, very soon.

The noises in the main ward quieted for the night. William sat up. He felt an uncharacteristic wish to shout for joy.

Instead he walked calmly to the window and put the key in the lock. The drop to the ground was about fifteen feet. If he broke an ankle, he'd just have to walk on it. He pushed open the window.

As an afterthought he crossed to the bed, reached under the mattress, and tucked the letter from Celine into his pocket. Might as well destroy the evidence that they had resumed contact, before she became his accomplice in a little something he had planned. A surprise for Elizabeth.

Then William felt someone staring at his back. Whirling, he saw insane black eyes peering through the tiny barred window in the door. It was one of the tunnel patients. "Where are you going?" the man whispered loudly.

William quickly thought about his options. Outside the locked door, the man was safe from strangling hands. "I've got to get out," William said soothingly. "But I'll be back for you."

"Come back and blow up those tunnels!" the man said forcefully and much too loudly.

"I've got to get the ammo," William whispered. "Then we'll blow up the tunnels together. But until then, you've got to be very, very quiet."

"Very quiet," the man whispered. "I won't make a sound." The face disappeared from the window.

William swallowed and wiped his sweating palms on the sheet. He waited a few seconds to see if the man would keep his word. William seemed to have lucked out. The ward remained deathly still.

With a quick motion he jackknifed himself up onto the windowsill. There wasn't room to turn and go feet first, he discovered. He'd just have to dive and hope he had enough time to tuck before his neck broke.

He hit the grass hard on one shoulder and the side of his head. For a second he lay stunned, a faint ringing in his ears. Then he slowly flattened out his body, waiting for his head to clear and to see if he had been detected.

Nothing. Only moonlight breaking through high clouds, silvering the dew on the well-kept, expansive lawns of the institution. William clutched the grass, feeling the delicious wetness cool his hands. Then he rose and ran to the woods. Staying in the cover of the trees, he headed for the parking lot, where his car was waiting.

William drove slowly through the parking lot and swung the Jag onto the main road, letting the tires screech just a little in celebration. This was it; no prison could hold him! His mind soared faster than the car, leaping over roads and mountains to the SVU campus.

Headlights loomed up the road. William froze, his hand gripping the gearshift. His breathing slowed, then ceased. Mechanically he dropped his speed. Who the hell could this be at one thirty in the morning? Had someone at the institution radioed an alarm?

William's hand crept to the tire jack waiting on the passenger seat. Anyone who tried to interfere with his plans was going to get his brains bashed in.

It was a garbage truck. Two men hung on to the side, eyeing him intently.

"Morning, doctor," one of them called.

"Good morning," William answered regally.

He managed to drive sedately until he rounded the first curve. Then he laughed aloud and slammed his foot down on the accelerator.

The wind blew his hair in glorious gusts of freedom. *Elizabeth, I am coming for you* . . .

Over the gorge he hit a hundred and ten.

When Elizabeth woke up, the garish orange lights of the school parking lot were shining in her eyes. Tom held her in his arms.

"Sleeping beauty," he said, brushing her hair from her face. "Want me to carry you?"

"I don't think so." Elizabeth rubbed her eyes and moved to her side of the seat. "People would think I was too messed up to walk. I have to think of my reputation."

"Right," Tom said, making a face. He locked up the Jeep. Then he turned to her, his expression very serious. "Will you come back to my room with me?" he asked softly, taking both of her hands.

Elizabeth searched his face. She saw whole-hearted love and deep respect. She imagined an entire night in his arms, lying in the velvety darkness, sharing all the delicious physical feelings she had only dreamed of. But . . .

She closed her eyes and slowly put her lips to his. She could smell the tangy scent of his breath. "Yes," she said. "I'll come back with you. But we can't . . . We really, really can't . . ."

"OK." Tom was looking at her solemnly. "I will control my hormones. I will try to behave."

"Just let me stop by my room for a minute to change," Elizabeth said slowly.

Tom smiled suggestively.

"No, you can't watch," she told him.

Several party people were still awake in her dorm. Two guys on Elizabeth's floor drunkenly greeted them.

Elizabeth flicked on the overhead light in her room. No Jessica, she saw to her surprise and dismay. Where could she be? Out with the late-night poetry crowd? As far as Elizabeth knew, it didn't exist. She punched on her desk lamp.

"Good Lord." Tom was staring at the ceiling. "What—"

"They're fruit flies," Elizabeth said, examining a fly that had committed hari-kari in her lamp. "This one is kind of cute, actually—it has curly wings. I wonder how they got in here."

"You got me," Tom said.

"Most of them seem to have met destiny around my lamp." Elizabeth picked up a fat fly and peered at it. "Hmmm. I wonder if a fruit fly invasion of my room has anything to do with a weird saxophonist serenading me at dawn?"

Tom raised an eyebrow. Elizabeth had told him about the morning concert. "Celine?"

"Who else?" Elizabeth agreed. "I'm going to have to put a stop to her tricks."

"How?" Tom asked, beginning to smile.

"I don't know yet," Elizabeth said, sweeping a few dozen dead flies from her desk to the floor. "I have to think about it. Maybe I'll saw all her shoes in half. No—that's not good enough. I'll have to devote some quality time to figuring out just what she deserves."

Tom squashed a couple of fruit flies crawling under the lamp.

"Don't hurt the little things," Elizabeth said, yanking open a drawer and rooting through her sweaters. "I hate to disappoint Celine, but I really don't feel like dealing with a bunch of flies tonight. Maybe we can catch them all in the morning and return them. But what I really want to know is, where's Jessica? She can't—" Elizabeth hesitated. "She isn't in some kind of trouble again, is she?" she finished.

"She probably went somewhere with a guy she met at the poetry recital," said Tom.

"See, that's exactly what I'm afraid of,"

205

Elizabeth said quickly. "It's kind of like living with a recovering alcoholic—what if she's fallen off the wagon and . . ."

"Stays out all night?" Tom finished. "I wouldn't panic yet, unless it turns out Mike McAllery has an identical twin too."

"I guess you're right," Elizabeth said with a sigh. "I think all the psychos and brutes are out of our lives now. Besides, I'm not her mother."

"Exactly," Tom said.

Tom waited outside while Elizabeth changed, then they walked over to Reid Hall and his room. Tom's floor was deserted.

"Where is everybody?" Tom wondered, opening his door. "I guess they're partied out." He crossed to his desk and lit a white candle.

Elizabeth gasped. The room was full of irises, crocuses, tiger lilies, and daisies. They were blooming across the desks and Tom's bed and swinging in baskets from the ceiling. *To My Inspiration, Elizabeth,* said a big heart-shaped sign in front of the mirror.

"I told Danny that our anniversary is tonight." Tom was grinning at her reaction. "That explains his absence." Suddenly he grew serious. He pulled Elizabeth into his arms, bringing them both onto the bed.

Elizabeth nestled beside him, and they held each other tight. She closed her eyes as Tom kissed her lips, then kissed down her throat to the top of her shirt. Slowly he undid the top button.

No, Elizabeth thought as a warm flood of feelings rushed through her. *We can't. We just can't.*

Her body didn't appear to be listening. Their kisses grew more passionate. *Stop it,* she ordered herself. Why was it every time her body was pressed against Tom's, it just refused to listen to her?

Stop it, she told herself again, totally unable to break away from him.

At that moment, the door to the room burst open and Danny poked his head in. "Anybody home?" he asked with a grin.

Tom jerked back, but Danny had vanished. Before Elizabeth could get over her shock enough to think, she heard Danny yell down the hall, "OK!"

The door flew open again and Danny, Isabella, Winston, Denise, Nina, and a German shepherd line-danced in. Danny was shaking maracas. They hadn't found a big poodle to dance with them, Elizabeth saw, but the German shepherd was hopping along in time to the beat, its paws on Winston's shoulders. Winston was rattling a tambourine. Suddenly the samba line stopped directly in front of Elizabeth and Tom. "Happy anniversary!" the dancers screamed all together. The dog barked.

"Bring on the chocolate-chip and peanut-butter ice cream!" Denise commanded, whirling her noisemaker. Nina darted outside the room, then came back with a stack of bowls and two half-gallons of ice cream. Danny lifted his pillow and retrieved a package of plastic spoons and a scoop.

Nina opened a carton of ice cream. "What flavor, party guy?" she asked Tom.

Tom was clearing his throat, unrumpling his shirt, trying to recover his composure. "Hey, either." He caught Danny's eye and shook his head. He couldn't help smiling. "You got me, buddy."

Elizabeth looked around at the delighted faces of their friends. She smiled resignedly. "Whose dog?" she asked, reaching out to pet it.

"It's the Sigma mascot," Isabella said, stroking its black-and-tan ears. "They've kind of made it one of the family."

Winston treated the dog to a dish of the peanut butter.

Hardly daring to, Elizabeth glanced at Tom. His laughing eyes met her own, and he squeezed her hand.

Saved again, she thought with a mixture of sadness and relief.

The Leaning Tower of Pisa swayed violently in a storm. Dark rain clouds swirled to the ground, sweeping up litter in brown mini torna-does. "Run!" Tisiano yelled over the gale. "Save yourself!"

Lila ran. But her body moved in slow motion, as if her feet were stuck in quicksand. The Tower whipped wildly back and forth. "It's going!" someone shouted. "Look out!"

Lila looked back as she kept trying to run. The trash flying through the air stung her arms and legs and she had trouble seeing. Somehow, though, she knew that when the Tower went, it would miss her, if only by inches.

The top of the Tower snapped off, sailing into the rotating winds. Then the rest of it fell and crashed down into gray rubble.

Now Lila knew why she couldn't run—she was on sand, of course, at the beach. The Mediterranean stretched before her. Tisiano waved from the Jet Ski. Lila cringed, because in about a second he was going to blow up.

Instead he pointed north—at the Italian Alps, Lila realized. She could see them clearly, even though they were more than a hundred miles away from where she was, in Genoa. Was it Genoa? The place felt different somehow. A small plane was climbing into the air near the mountains, trying to cross.

The plane is too small to make it, Lila thought in Italian. *I've got to stop it. If only I could run fast enough.*

The plane wavered. Then it began to plunge.

The plane crashed in a shattering explosion. Streaks of red flame and black smoke rapidly devoured the icy white mountainside.

Lila woke, gasping. She slowly sat up, her hands at her throat.

"It was only a dream," she whispered.

But this one was different. Almost every night in her sleep she replayed the scene of Tisiano's death. She was used to that. Sometimes she awoke screaming; sometimes just shaking.

This dream was worse, because she had no idea what it meant. "I need a glass of water," she said to herself.

Lila padded out to the kitchen, opened the refrigerator, and poured a glass of mineral water. The clock said quarter of two. Lila nodded. The dreams always came after midnight, sometimes more than once.

The uneasy feeling from the dream lingered with her. That could be a sign that when she slept again, she would return to it. Maybe she should hope she could get back into the dream, so that she could find out what it meant.

Chapter Thirteen

A lone fruit fly circled, dove, and crashed into the desk lamp, the only light in the room. Elizabeth watched it idly, her face in her hands. She was thinking about her evening with Tom.

Love, she thought. *So this is what it feels like. It's simple, really. You're just completely sure that person is the one you want to be with as much as possible: in your thoughts, talking, probably in bed. Maybe forever . . .* She sighed and pushed back her hair. The quiet of the room was beginning to bother her. She had gotten back from Tom's half an hour ago, and it was two in the morning. Where was Jessica?

The small stack of today's mail caught her eye. She picked it up and sorted through it. There was a letter addressed to Jessica in an official-looking envelope, two catalogs for Elizabeth from outdoor-wear companies, and a plain white envelope with just Elizabeth's name on it.

Elizabeth ripped open the envelope and unfolded the single sheet of paper inside. The familiar black, block letters jumped out at her: "I am coming for you." Elizabeth looked at the message, her mouth set. This was *not* from Tom; he had said so. She felt a flutter of fear in her stomach. There was something frightening about the writer's anonymity.

"It must be from Todd," she murmured, although that still seemed unlikely. Todd had always been direct with her—sticking unsigned little notes under the door was hardly his style.

But then, she felt that she hardly knew Todd anymore. He certainly didn't seem much like the intelligent, *sober* Todd Wilkins she had gone out with in high school.

The next moment someone started pounding on the door. Elizabeth stared. The door was actually vibrating on its hinges from the blows. "Stop it!" she shouted.

The hammering stopped. Elizabeth marched to the door and opened it. She wasn't surprised to see Todd.

Elizabeth hadn't seen him since last night, after the saxophonist's touching rendition of her song, "I Can't Believe That You're in Love with Me." Then the concert had ended, and Tom had leaped up with clenched fists and faced

Todd. Elizabeth had barely been able to get Tom away before a fight started.

"I'm coming in, Liz," Todd said grimly, and pushed past her before she could stop him. "You can't stand me up again."

Elizabeth's heart beat faster with the sudden realization that she had promised to meet Todd for coffee tonight.

Todd walked slowly toward her. He seemed slightly unsteady on his feet, and as he came closer Elizabeth was aware of how big he was. She backed away until she was up against the door. For just a second fear shivered up her spine.

This is Todd, she reminded herself. *Todd, your old boyfriend. You can't possibly be afraid of him. Besides . . . what will happen if he knows you're afraid?*

Then he stopped about two paces away. Elizabeth felt relieved, then angry. She opened her mouth to tell him how she felt, but Todd interrupted her.

"Liz, look. I—I miss you," Todd said quietly. "I wanted to see you. I don't think . . ." Todd looked away for a second. "I don't think life is possible for me without you. I love you, and I'll do anything to get you back—anything," he said. His voice broke on the last word.

Elizabeth took a step toward him to put her hand on Todd's shoulder. She knew how it felt to have a broken heart. She wanted to be the best friend to him she could.

Todd pulled her roughly to him and kissed her on the lips.

Elizabeth yanked herself away. "Todd, stop it!" she almost screamed.

Todd's eyes filled with tears. He sank into her desk chair. "I'm sorry," he whispered.

Elizabeth tried to get control of herself. Her face was hot, and her heart was racing. *He's drunk,* she thought. *He probably won't even remember this in the morning.*

She could still feel his lips on hers. Her anger rose again. "I want you to leave me alone, Todd. Don't come over here, and stop sending me notes!" she yelled.

Todd looked at her. "I haven't sent you any notes."

Elizabeth peered at him suspiciously. Suddenly she realized two things: that he wasn't as drunk as she'd thought, and that he was telling the truth. Todd had never lied to her, and he wasn't now.

She seized the note on her desk and handed it to him. "Then how do you explain this?"

Todd shook his head. "That's not my handwriting. Anyway, why would I write you a note saying I'm coming for you when I'm already here?"

"To drive me crazy?" Elizabeth suggested,

her expression softening a little as her anger and fear had died down. She couldn't help it. Todd had acted outrageously tonight, but he hadn't always been this way. She didn't believe he would ever really be a threat to her.

Todd smiled back, but it was the saddest smile she had ever seen. He glanced down at the floor. He was going to cry; she could tell.

Elizabeth wanted so much to say the right thing. But she knew there was nothing. Nothing she could say, and nothing she could do.

"So if you're not sending me the notes and Tom's not, who is?" she said, more to herself than to him.

"Some poor crazed sucker who loves you?" Todd suggested.

Jessica smiled seductively over her third cup of espresso. "So you like women with tattoos?" she said.

James laughed. "Just because I've got a tattoo doesn't mean everyone should. I saw a woman at the beach last summer who had green and blue snakes from her belly to her neck. I thought that was going a little far."

"I would get something more subtle." Jessica put down her cup. "Maybe just a few stars above my wrist. Or a rose on my ankle. A lot of women have tattoos these days—they're very chic."

"I volunteer to hold your hand while you get it done," James said, rolling down his sleeve over the green dolphin tattoo on his forearm. "It hurts like hell."

"Maybe everyone isn't as sensitive as you." Jessica smiled into his eyes. He smiled back. He looked more like James Bond than ever. James Bond with a tattoo.

Jessica was having a wonderful time. Here she was back in the coffeehouse, one of her first college hangouts, with a handsome new man who was treating her as politely and gently as if she were a glass slipper. Best of all, even though they'd met at a poetry recital, the conversation hadn't stayed stuck on poets for long. They had been chatting easily for hours. "I'll let you know when I make my appointment for tattooing," she said.

"Do that." James hesitated. "I don't know how you're going to take this, but . . ."

"But what?" Jessica encouraged him. In her experience, guys always finished that opener with a very complimentary remark, like, "The instant I saw you, I realized that you were the only woman for me" or "That first day of chem class, I knew I wanted to marry you."

"I know you're married."

Married. That was what James had said. *I know you're married*.

Jessica took a deep breath, trying to refocus

her thoughts. "Not exactly," she said, finding she couldn't meet his gaze. She cleared her throat. "My marriage is going to be annulled soon. But unfortunately that won't be the end of my relationship with my husband. Ex-husband, I mean. I want to help in his rehabilitation." Her voice cracked. "Because he's in very bad shape after . . . the accident. The accidental shooting."

Jessica finally looked up, her blue-green eyes filled with tears. She was afraid of what she would see in James's face. Pity. Disgust. Scorn. But she saw none of that. His expression was open and understanding.

"I heard about what happened," he said sympathetically. He held up both hands. "Hey, we don't have to talk about it. I thought you might want to, if you haven't got a friendly ear to listen. It's just—I really like you, and I want to get to know you better—" Here came the compliment, but she wasn't in the mood for it anymore.

". . . and I watch you in chem more than I watch the professor," he finished.

"No, you don't," Jessica scoffed, trying to feel as flirtatious as she had thirty seconds ago. "You premeds are all alike. You sit in the front row, where you couldn't possibly see me or anyone else, and you don't even take a breath unless Professor Taschek says 'All right, class, ready—*breathe*!'"

217

He laughed. He did have an awfully nice laugh. "OK, maybe I just think about you in class," James acknowledged. "But if a premed sacrifices chemistry time to think about a woman, it means he's willing to die at the stake for her."

Jessica swallowed. His cheer-up tactics should be working on her, but they weren't. She knew she shouldn't be here. She didn't deserve it. Where was Mike? Sitting with all the lights out in his apartment, barely able to move, fantasizing about the days when Jessica had loved him.

Jessica got up hastily, blinking back tears. "I can't stay," she said. "I'm sorry. Thank you for the espresso." *And for making me forget my problems for a whole evening,* she thought. A tear ran down her cheek.

"A good blues band is going to play in about ten minutes. Why don't you stay?" James asked, reaching for her hand. "We can talk, or just shut up and listen to the music."

He thinks he was tactless asking about Mike, Jessica thought. *He wasn't. He's such a perfectly sweet guy.* "I can't," she said. "I really appreciate the offer, though." Jessica was surprised that she was being so sincere. Usually when she was bailing on a guy, she said that sort of thing without meaning it at all. "Maybe another time."

James smiled. "Either we could go out, or—I

don't know if you need help in chem, but if you do, I could help. Or we could just study together. Cheer each other on."

I can study with him, can't I? Jessica asked her conscience. *Yes,* it seemed to say. "Wonderful; I'd love to." Jessica put on her best cheerleader smile but withdrew her hand. "Excuse me."

"Sure," James said. Jessica could feel his eyes following her out the door.

She hurried to the pay phone in the little anteroom between the eating area and outside, and dug into her pockets for change. Of course these were Elizabeth's pants and of course Elizabeth had one quarter in the right-front pocket, ready for an emergency call. "What a sister," Jessica murmured, quickly feeding the quarter into the wall telephone and punching Mike's number.

The phone buzzed in her ear. Six rings. Eight rings. Twelve. "Why isn't he answering?" Jessica wondered aloud. "Has he gone out? *Does* he go out? Maybe he doesn't pick up the phone at all. It's late, somebody should be there. Where's Steven?"

Jessica finally clanked down the receiver. After twenty rings she had gotten no answer. What was going on?

Todd stalked into Alex's room without waiting for her to answer the door. He began to pace from the window to her desk.

Alex sighed. She poured him a scotch, straight up, from her open bottle. "Here," she said.

"I might as well drink." Todd took the glass from her and drank half the scotch in a gulp. Alex had never seen him look so grim. "At least you're always here," he said, wiping his mouth with his hand.

"I'm here for you," she whispered.

"No, I mean in your room." Todd sat on her desk. "You never go out. You really should try to have some fun."

You only go out to pester Elizabeth, Alex thought sourly. *It's not like you're going out on the town, either.*

"I'm not into fun anymore," she said aloud. She pointed to a pile of books on the desk. "I've been reading about Buddhism." Actually, she had read only three pages before she had thrown herself back on her bed and started crying about Mark, but at least she had done something that Elizabeth Wakefield would approve of. Elizabeth, success queen of SVU.

Alex was totally sick of Elizabeth. Even though she had been an Elizabeth Wakefield wannabe all through high school, Alex had never beaten Elizabeth at anything.

If only something bad would happen to her for once, Alex thought. *Really bad, so she would know how it feels.*

Alex felt guilty. She glanced at Todd. He was holding up his glass and looking through the clear amber of the scotch. She remembered back to the beginning of the semester when bad things *were* happening to Elizabeth.

"Elizabeth's schizo these days," he said. "She yells at me, then smiles at me, until I don't know what the hell I'm supposed to think."

"Sounds like Elizabeth," Alex said in a hard voice. It sounded like Mark, too: totally unpredictable, completely inconsiderate. She hadn't heard from Mark. Finally yesterday, scotchless, she had forced herself to look in the mirror and tell herself that she never would hear from him. Then she had given herself permission to get drunk.

"We went out for years and now she barely lets me in the door," Todd went on. Alex was tired of listening to the same old dirge, but at least it reminded her that she wasn't the only one who had screwed up.

Todd tossed down the rest of his drink. "I'm scared, Alex. I've never been scared like this before. It's like I know somewhere in my mind that I can't get Elizabeth back, but I can't stop trying. I can't accept that I made such a huge mistake—she just has to come back to me. Pour me another drink, would you? It helps."

It did help. Alex wasn't sure which kind—gin, bourbon, scotch, tequila, or rum—helped

221

most. *We're such losers,* she thought bitterly.

"Same as before?" she asked, holding out the scotch bottle by its neck.

"If only she was," Todd said wearily. "Liz has changed, at least toward me. I guess her success with those journalism stories went to her head. I should be glad I helped her out by being a corrupt jock."

Alex handed him a glass of straight bourbon this time.

"I don't understand why she hangs with Tom Watts," Todd said. His voice had a real edge now. "Watts just uses Elizabeth's talent. What has he ever done? He's a nobody."

Alex silently poured herself a glass of tequila. This was potent stuff. She'd discovered it yesterday in a liquor store when she'd heard a couple of frat guys joking about its transcendent powers. Alex doubted if Todd wanted her real opinion about why Elizabeth was seeing Tom Watts: because he was one of the most desirable, best-looking guys on campus.

Of course, so was Todd. Alex looked over at him again. Even drunk, slouched on her desk, he was very nice to look at. And it was hard to imagine having a good time with someone as straight-arrow and dedicated to journalism as Tom.

On the other hand, being dedicated straight arrows seemed to work for Tom and Elizabeth, while nothing she did worked at all. "I've been thinking about changing my name back to Enid," she said dully.

"Are you joking?" Todd stared at her. "Why would you do that? You're not . . . her anymore."

"I'm not, but maybe I should be." Alex sighed. Tears were close. Why was she crying all the time? Why couldn't her life be some other way?

Todd moved to her bed and patted the space next to him. "I don't want you to go back to being Enid," he said. "You're a lot sweeter and sexier than she used to be."

Alex smiled at him through her tears and gulped her drink. She sat beside him, and he put his arm around her shoulders.

"This is like old times, isn't it?" she said. "We've always been great friends."

"You are a real friend, Alex." Todd put down his bourbon. "You've proved that."

Todd turned her face toward his. Alex felt the burn and blur of the tequila suddenly hit hard. *Damn right I'm not Enid,* she thought.

"Let's not talk about them," she whispered breathlessly. "I want to keep feeling the way I do now."

Without warning Todd's mouth came down on hers. Alex passionately kissed him back as he pulled her body close to his.

*   *   *

"So where were you?" Elizabeth asked, twisting around in her desk chair. "Out with a guy?"

Jessica scowled and tossed her bag on the floor. Elizabeth preferred what she called the direct approach. Jessica would have called it the nosy approach. What was Elizabeth doing anyway, parked at her desk at two in the morning, surrounded by flies? Jessica was a little tired. She really wished Elizabeth would lie down and go to sleep instead of interrogating her.

"Don't you want to know how the poetry reading went?" Jessica countered.

"I'm sure it went fine." Elizabeth yawned.

Jessica stared at her. "You don't even want to know if I forgot every single line of the poem and ruined the reading?"

Elizabeth snapped her mouth shut. "Did something go wrong?"

"No, that was later," Jessica said. "I had everybody in tears with the poem."

"Is there anything I need to know? Like conversations you had as me afterward?"

"I didn't talk to any of those geeks." It was Jessica's turn to yawn. "I escaped the instant it was over."

"With a guy," Elizabeth prompted.

"You don't let up, do you?" Jessica demanded, marching to the mirror and grabbing her hairbrush.

"Who was he?"

"Nobody." Jessica picked a dead fly from the brush handle and began stroking her hair energetically.

"A cute nobody?" Elizabeth persisted.

Jessica put down the brush with a groan. "All right. I had a heavy date at the coffeehouse with a gorgeous premed from my chemistry class. His name is James Montgomery. We talked about Mike's paralyzed condition and my annulment. I'm sure James can't wait to go out with me again after spending such a fascinating evening." Jessica's voice wavered a little in spite of herself.

"Hmmm," Elizabeth said thoughtfully. "I don't know James."

"You wouldn't; he's a Sigma."

Her twin made a sour face. "I actually do know most of the Sigmas. If half of the Sigmas had almost killed you, you might not rush into dating the other half."

"James didn't have a thing to do with that," Jessica assured her. Had he? They hadn't discussed it this evening. But Elizabeth knew the names of all the Sigmas who had tried to kill her, and she hadn't flinched when Jessica mentioned James.

Elizabeth still had that pinched look of disapproval.

"Just because he's a Sigma doesn't mean he knew anything about the secret society," Jessica

225

pointed out. "That's why they called it a secret society."

"Quitting that frat would have been the only decent thing to do after the truth came out, whether he was involved or not," Elizabeth said righteously. "When they were filling up the pit under the house with concrete, I could have made a list of Sigma brothers who deserved a nice set of concrete shoes."

"James is a gentleman," Jessica informed her. "He's not into killing women in basements."

"Glad to hear it," Elizabeth retorted. "But if he's waiting to hear about the annulment, this might be good news." She handed Jessica a letter.

Jessica grabbed the envelope and stared down at it as though it had fangs.

"Oh, God," she said. The hand clutching the envelope trembled. "Liz, this is from the lawyer. It's going to say the final word about if I got the annulment or not."

"Open it," Elizabeth urged, getting up from her desk.

Jessica didn't move.

"I'll do it." Elizabeth reached for it.

"No!" Jessica snatched the letter away. "I'm just trying to think what I'm going to do if the answer is no. Drive ninety miles an hour off a cliff?"

"Then you'll have to go the divorce route,"

Elizabeth said quickly. "It won't be the end of the world."

"Yeah, I guess the world ended when Mike got shot," Jessica said softly.

Her sister frowned. "It did not. Jess, please just open the letter."

Jessica took a deep breath, then frantically tore open the envelope. Her eyes scanned the lines, almost unable to make sense of them. Then she gasped.

"Jess?" Elizabeth looked genuinely scared.

"My marriage has been annulled," Jessica said slowly. She shook the letter. "It's really over."

"Great, Jess." Elizabeth hugged her. "You've been through a lot of suffering to get to this."

Jessica hugged her back. But then she dropped the letter. It fluttered quietly to the floor and lay facedown.

"What is it?" Elizabeth asked anxiously.

"It's not over," Jessica said with a sigh. "Who am I kidding?"

"What do you mean? The marriage is annulled—it never really happened." Elizabeth looked at her quizzically.

"But the marriage isn't all that Mike and I had," Jessica tried to explain. "We were in love. I can't just desert him when he's down. I should keep on seeing him and helping him as long as he lives," she finished. "So should Steven."

Elizabeth frowned. "Jess, I don't really know if that would be best," she said. "You'll still be living two lives, trying to take care of him and be a college student. . . . Don't you think you have to let go?"

"That would be running away," Jessica said, trying to sound more certain than she felt.

"No, it wouldn't," Elizabeth insisted. "Mike and Steven are responsible for their own lives. Steven was ordered by the court to help Mike because he was partially responsible for what happened. This annulment means you aren't involved anymore."

"I am too. Nothing has changed." The tears in Jessica's eyes spilled over.

"Jess, how is your hanging around Mike going to help him, when it's all over between you? Does he even want you to?"

Jessica shook her head and grabbed a tissue from the box on her desk. "No," she said, her voice muffled.

"Well, then," Elizabeth said, in an infuriatingly logical voice.

"I can't desert him!" Jessica said angrily.

"But you're gone already."

"Our love is gone." Jessica began to cry into the tissue. But at the same time, she felt relieved. Elizabeth patted her back.

Finally Jessica looked up. *I've got to look at the positive side of things,* she thought. *Being on good terms with Elizabeth again. Lila back home. Passing chemistry with James Montgomery.*

"Better?" Elizabeth asked with a smile.

"Much." Jessica tossed back her hair and returned her twin's smile. "There's just one thing . . ." She batted down a fruit fly with the paper she was holding. "Are these new friends of yours going to live with us?"

But Elizabeth hadn't even heard her. Her gaze was fixed on a sheet of paper slowly, noiselessly sliding under the door. Without thinking, she went over and picked it up.

Elizabeth felt her heart hammering in her chest before she'd even read the words.

Not long now, was written on the paper in a heavy black scrawl.

She threw open the door and looked down the hall. No one was there.

Wind chimes blew somewhere far away. Peaceful images floated before Steven's eyes: his parents standing in the middle of the driveway, waving him off to college; his seven-year-old sisters bent over a mud puddle and poking sticks in it; Billie laughing, pulling him by the hand to the homecoming dance last fall.

The grass waved gently, emerald green and warmed by the sun. The brilliant blue bowl of the sky was free of clouds or smog. Steven raced after Billie, laughing too. *Wait!* he called.

Suddenly Billie looked over her shoulder, her eyes pleading. "Steven, *please!* You have to turn off the gas! You're dying!"

Billie wavered, then disappeared into the mist. "Don't go!" Steven yelled. But that wasn't mist. It was smoke, something thick that choked his lungs. He realized what the visions meant—that he was going to heaven, or what he wanted heaven to be like. He was dying. He had to . . . Steven forced himself back up into the waves of nausea and consciousness. The gas. He had to shut it off.

Do it. Get up! screamed one corner of his mind, the tiny part out of reach of the cloying, sickening smell of the gas.

But he just couldn't make his heavy, tired limbs move.

The phone rang. Chimes? Someone was screaming. *"Wakefield! Get out of here,* now. *This place is going to blow!"*

Mike. Mike was paralyzed and depending on Steven to save him. Or was that Billie's voice?

Steven summoned up the last of his strength. Billie . . . he could almost see her, a shadow perfectly outlined in the gray-black air. His hands lifted, reaching. Then they fell. The screaming seemed louder and closer, more desperate.

I'm sorry, Billie, he thought dizzily as the mist surrounded him again. *I won't make it. I wanted to try one last time for you . . . because, did I ever tell you? I love you so. . . .*

The blackness came down like a final curtain.

Your friends at Sweet Valley High have had their world turned upside down!

Meet one person with a power so evil, so dangerous, that it could destroy the entire world of Sweet Valley!

A Night to Remember, the book that starts it all, is followed by a six book series filled with romance, drama and suspense.

- ♡ 29309-5 A NIGHT TO REMEMBER (Magna Edition) ..$3.99/4.99 Can.
- ♡ 29852-6 THE MORNING AFTER #95 ....$3.50/4.50 Can.
- ♡ 29853-4 THE ARREST #96...$3.50/4.50 Can.
- ♡ 29854-2 THE VERDICT #97 ....$3.50/4.50 Can.
- ♡ 29855-0 THE WEDDING #98...$3.50/4.50 Can.
- ♡ 29856-9 BEWARE THE BABYSITTER #99.....................$3.50/4.50 Can.
- ♡ 29857-7 THE EVIL TWIN #100 ....$3.99/4.99 Can.